CHARON'S EYES

had found them again, and unless Kayla acted quickly, she was doomed. Without asking permission, she grabbed hold of Keller's mind and used it to augment her own mindpower.

Suddenly, a huge demon towered over them, a ritual warrior with bloody runes engraved into his cheeks and forehead. His lipless mouth opened to reveal pointed teeth as sharp as swords. His eyes blazed with terrible fires. And where his chest and guts should have been was instead a cage filled with gaunt and hollow-eyed prisoners. Their faces were those of the members of Charon's Eyes.

Kayla had the thing exhale mind-numbing energy, scrambling the brains of the other empaths. The creature set tiny fire imps dancing in their eyes, plucking at their deepest fears, sending them into mounting panic.

Out of the shadows came lumbering jailers without eyes, reaching with spidery hands to scoop them up and imprison them in the demon warrior's chest. . . .

Be sure to read all the books
in this action-packed
DAW science fiction series from
KAREN HABER

WOMAN WITHOUT A SHADOW (Book One)
THE WAR MINSTRELS (Book Two)
SISTER BLOOD (Book Three)

SISTER BLOOD

KAREN HABER

DAW BOOKS, INC.
DONALD A. WOLLHEIM, FOUNDER
375 Hudson Street, New York, NY 10014

ELIZABETH R. WOLLHEIM
SHEILA E. GILBERT
PUBLISHERS

Cover art by Romas Kukalis.

DAW Book Collectors No. 1029.

First Printing, August 1996
1 2 3 4 5 6 7 8 9

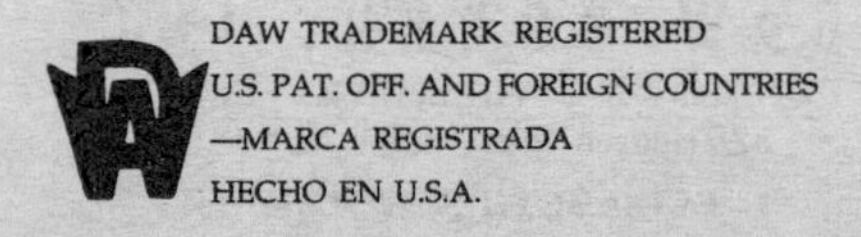

PRINTED IN THE U.S.A.

For my mother,
who always believed,
with my love and gratitude

"In a certain sense, every single human soul has more meaning and value than the whole of history with its empires, its wars and revolutions, its blossoming and fading civilizations."

—Nicholas Berdyaev

Chapter One

The planet Styx had seen difficult birth, and its early life could be read in many volcanic scars which swirled across its icebound surface.

Inside, it was habitable. Barely.

Natural tunnels had been expanded by the patient work of miners long gone.

The planet would have been unremarkable save for the unusual nature of the crystals found within its heart.

Mindstones. Red-blue and bronze gems with acid-green striations that amplified esper powers and were coveted in every corner of the galaxy. Even more coveted was the by-product of mindstone mining: mindsalt. Dangerous. Addictive. Consumed in liquid, it produced unpredictable mental effects. Mindsalt could give euphoria or agony. With time and continual use, it hollowed a person out, left nothing but a vestigial personality, a shell.

Styx had been a matter of recent concern to Kayla

John Reed, known to some as Kate N. Shadow. She was returning to her birthplace after many years' absence, but the homecoming would not be joyous. She was going to meet her old enemy, Yates Keller. Only one of them would walk away. She had vowed it upon the deaths of her parents years ago, and on all the blood she had spilled since then.

* * *

The stars were a familiar sight to Kayla, companions to her many journeys in the dark vacuum of space. She was accustomed to charting new routes through unknown places. But the route she charted now was one that she knew only too well, and the place she was going was the place she had come from.

Styx. Would she truly walk through those cold and shining tunnels once again, weaving her way between glittering black stalagmites that thrust up from the cave floor like dark teeth in a giant mouth?

This would be a solo landing, but en route she had the comfort of her companion, Iger, and the dalkoi, Third Child. Twice now, Iger had tried to convince her to allow him to come with her into the heart of Styx.

"No," she had replied, and continued to reply each time he asked. The instructions she had received from her old enemy, Yates Keller, were explicit: "If you'd like to see your friends again, come meet me on Styx. Alone."

"I'll be watching for you," Keller had said. "Come in a single shuttle. One passenger. Anything else will get blasted out of the sky."

Kayla was going to Styx because she had no choice. Keller had kidnapped her close friends, the crew of the good ship *Falstaff*: Salome, Barabbas, and Arsobades. It was her fault they had fallen into his hands. She had to save them. Nothing, nothing was as important.

In a way, she looked forward to grappling with Keller and settling accounts once and for all. Her parents' deaths were on his head, and her comrades' misfortune. Yates Keller had a bad habit of destroying everything that he touched.

But not me, she thought. *He tried, and failed, and I've only gotten stronger. This time I'll finish him. Finish him and get out of this godforsaken system once and for all. Put light-years between me and the double suns of Cavinas, take a one-way zigzag course through jumpspace, good-bye. And bring along as many of the War Minstrels as care to come with me.*

The War Minstrels. She smiled at the thought: a ragtag group of former prisoners who had shaped up into a formidable fighting force, bringing an end to the despotic rule of Prime Minister Pelleas Karlson, and forcing the reform of the Trade Alliance along fair trade practices. She had led them through the darkness. Soon she would lead them toward the light.

Keller first, though. It had always been leading to this, an inevitable collision between them, from the first time they met, two green kids in the tunnels of Styx. A fitting return indeed.

"We're beyond Xenobe's orbit," Iger announced. "And Mac is still begging us to come back."

"Maintain radio silence," Kayla said. "He knows I have to do this."

The gas-giant planet, Xenobe, filled the viewscreen with its purple bulk. Barely visible was the twinkling mass that was St. Ilban, Xenobe's only moon, the center of the Cavinas System, and the heart of the Trade Alliance.

* * *

Lyle MacKenzie paced the communications center in the Crystal Palace in the heart of Vardalia, capital city of St. Ilban and the Trade Alliance. The chief commander of the War Minstrels in Kayla's absence, MacKenzie was a tall rangy man who moved with sizzling energy. As he strode from one side of the room to the other, his bristling gingery hair flew upward in tendrils. Pausing, he snapped his fingers in irritation. "Get me their frequency again, goddammit. Get me the *Antimony*'s frequency, and Kate!"

"We never lost their frequency," Mepal Tarlinger,

the com board operator, shot back. "We're sending. But they're not sending back."

"Damn her!" MacKenzie said. "Why is she running off on this crazy mission?"

"With us left behind, holding the fort for Her Highness. As usual." The voice, a deep basso, belonged to Merrick the Blackbird, former bounty hunter, most recently a commander of the War Minstrels. Large of body, dark of mien, Merrick leaned his imposing bulk into a webseat and placed his booted feet upon the com board frame. He watched his smaller colleague with barely concealed amusement and friendly contempt. "What's the matter, Mac? You really think we can't cope without her?"

"That's not the point, Blackbird. We need her here. People trust her. They listen to her."

"They listen to us, too. Or else." Merrick slapped the disruptor he wore on his belt.

MacKenzie glared at him. "That's exactly my point. People listen to her without fearing her. Besides, she's throwing herself into God-knows-what kind of dangerous situation."

"That's her choice, isn't it?" Merrick said. "Kate's a big girl, Mac. And she asked us to look after things. So relax. I can think of worse postings. We're in the heart of the Three Systems, with more food and drink than I've seen in a year, every comfort a man could want, and then some. *You* might need Katie." His gaze darkened. "I sure as hell don't."

MacKenzie stared at his colleague, irritation igniting in his hazel eyes. "You think that running this place is going to be fun? A real cakewalk?"

Merrick gave him a sharp, mirthless smile. "I think it can be. But I didn't exactly have cake in mind." He rose, nodded. "You want me, I'll be in the Amethyst suite."

"But those were Karlson's rooms."

"Were."

Before MacKenzie could protest further, Merrick the Blackbird put his booted feet on the floor and swaggered out of the door.

Damn the man! MacKenzie had no great love for his cocommander and knew the enmity was returned. For the sake of the War Minstrels and Kate, he would force himself to get along with Merrick, but the sooner he could jettison that bastard and get back to the peace and quiet of space, the better.

* * *

Aboard the *Antimony*, Kayla was remembering:

In the middle of the room, a cloud of light coalesced, slowly forming itself into a holoimage of a dark-eyed, dark-haired man, good-looking in a slick, arrogant manner.

Yates Keller.

"I knew you'd come here," the holoimage had said.

Kayla remembered how tempted she had been to put a laser bolt right through the replica of that smug face.

"You're looking for me, Kayla, aren't you? If not, you should be."

The image had blurred for a moment and quickly re-formed to show perfect ebony features framed by swirling golden hair. Amber eyes stared defiantly. Salome.

And the image had faded, to be replaced by the faces of Salome's lover, bearded leonine Barabbas, and his friend, the red-haired minstrel and weapons master, Arsobades. Then they were gone and the picture blurred one more time, to re-form around Keller's grinning visage.

"Obviously, I've got something that I think you want. And you have something I want. You know what I'm talking about, Kayla. The Mindstar. I want it."

The Mindstar. A huge, unusually potent mindstone which several people had killed for—and been killed by owning. Kayla had put herself at great risk to find it, had nearly been overmastered by the thing, and only with the help of Iger and Third Child had she managed to use it. The use she had put it to had destroyed the Mindstar's power although the stone had remained intact. But Yates Keller didn't know that.

"Meet me, Kayla. The Alliance can be ours. You

weren't meant to be a rebel. Join me. Save your friends and yourself. I'm offering you much more than they can."

The image swirled back into mist and dissipated. But the threat it had made reverberated in Kayla's mind: *—If you try any tricks, I'll begin killing your friends, one by one.*

Kayla could repeat that part of the message in her sleep.

So Yates Keller wanted the Mindstar, did he? Then she would bring it, oh, yes, count on it. Nothing could stop her.

* * *

On the viewscreen, Styx was growing, changing from a speck of light indistinct from all the other gems glowing in the night sky to a larger, more specific orb. It filled the viewscreen with its greenish bulk until Kayla could see her reflected image upon it: pointed chin, determined mouth, green eyes, and red hair sheared in a short, boyish cut. Kayla's face, superimposed on Styx. A planet's face. She grinned and the planet grinned with her.

And Yates Keller was waiting there.

The grin deepened, became feral.

"Kayla, we have to talk."

She jumped. It was rare that her companion, Iger, could sneak up on her: her empathic powers prevented many surprises. But she had been so absorbed in the image of her home world that she had not heard Iger's footsteps.

She smiled at him, admiring yet again the strong lines of his face, the blue eyes, and the long blond hair pulled back behind his neck. She squeezed his arm affectionately. "What's up?"

"It's Third Child. Something's wrong with that dalkoi."

Kayla's smile faltered. "What do you mean?"

"She's not interested in eating."

Not interested in eating? It was Third Child's favorite activity. "That *is* strange. And alarming."

"I know. She doesn't come when I call. She doesn't respond when I address her."

"Let me try." Kayla was on her feet and moving quickly toward the door.

"She's in her quarters. Good luck."

Kayla approached the dalkoi's room cautiously, buzzing first to be admitted. The door opened and she saw the two-limbed dalkoi sitting curled upon the bunk, sleepy-eyed, barely acknowledging her presence. Yet again the oddness of its appearance struck her: the triangular head, rounded body, violet flesh, lipless mouth, and huge purple eyes.

"Third Child, may I use mindspeech?"

There was no response, which she took to mean yes. Odd, that the dalkoi didn't respond.

—*Dear friend, what's wrong?*

—Wrong? Nothing is wrong.

The mental emanations were familiar, and yet there was something altered and strange about them.

—You sound peculiar.

—Peculiar is not the correct word. I am paan-hansi.

—Paan-hansi? What does that mean?

—In your language: with child.

—Are you joking?

—Why would I joke about this?

—But how? How is it possible? Don't you require a breeding group? Liagean foods?

—Usually. But in ususual circumstances, we dalkoi are adaptive. We change.

—You do? Then who were your breeding partners?

—You. And Iger.

—What?

Kayla sat down on the bunk, her mind refusing to take in the new situation.

Calmly, Third Child continued to explain.

—My people can breed parthenogenetically, under great mental stimulation from other species.

—I don't believe this, Third Child. It can't be true!

Stunned, Kayla cut off their mindlink. She needed time to consider this.

Third Child, pregnant, with a little help from Iger and herself? It was too weird, too unbelievable. Third Child's sense of whimsy was getting out of hand. Perhaps she was trying to get more attention from her friends, feeling neglected. Yes, that had to be it.

Irritated, Kayla mindspoke the dalkoi once more.

—Look, I know that Iger and I have been pretty busy, preoccupied with getting to Styx, but it's unnecessary to pull a stunt like this to get our attention.

The vehemence of the dalkoi's response overwhelmed her.

—I am pulling no stunt. Don't condescend to me, Kayla. Look, for once, at what is squarely before you!

Kayla recoiled. Third Child had never addressed her in such anger. Something had changed. Could what the dalkoi said be true? Was she pregnant?

—I'm sorry, Third Child, but it's so difficult for me to believe this.

—Believe what you like. The fact remains.

Kayla wanted more time to think this through. But there was no time, with Styx looming ever larger. She hit the com link, hard.

"Iger! Get down here!"

"Katie, somebody has got to steer this bus."

"Put it on autopilot."

"You sound upset."

"Just get here."

He was there faster than she would have thought possible. Strands of his dark blond hair were escaping from the thong with which he had tied them. His blue eyes were wide with apprehension. "Okay, I'm here. What's happened? What is it?"

"Third Child is going to have a baby."

"Very funny."

"I'm not joking."

Iger took a step backward. "How can she have offspring?"

"I don't know. That's what she told me."

"Third Child?" Iger said. "Third Child, is this true?"

Third Child gave a languid chirrup of affirmation.

"Are you sure?"

Another chirrup.

"Wait, Iger. There's more." Kayla's voice sounded thin in her own ears. "She says that we're the parents. You. And me. We three."

"What? You can't be serious."

"I find it kind of hard to believe myself. But that's what she says. All of our mental connection and such seems to have, well, stimulated her."

"She's got to be mistaken," Iger shook his head. "I've never heard of such a thing."

"How many dalkois spend their time off Liage, away from their breeding groups?" Kayla asked. "Maybe this is the only documented time that this has happened."

"You're taking this pretty calmly," Iger said.

"It's shock, not calm. But you know all about dalkois, don't you?"

"I don't know anything about playing midwife to one!"

"Better start learning. How long is their gestation period?"

"It varies, depending upon the security of their surroundings and food supply."

"How long has she been pregnant?"

"Who knows? She probably doesn't."

"I thought you were an expert on dalkois."

"You thought wrong."

"Then we've got to get her medical attention."

"What for? She looks healthy."

"But we don't know what to expect. What if she needs special food and such?"

"You think a doctor will know? Most of them have never even seen a dalkoi before."

"You've got a point." Kayla subsided, thinking. "Well, get the knowbot to research Liagean exobiology records. And try to keep an eye on Third Child while I'm on Styx."

"Of course. But who'll keep an eye on you?"

The telemetry klaxon went off, hoarsely announcing their final approach to Styx, and there wasn't time to consider the dietary needs of pregnant dalkois or much of anything else.

Chapter Two

MacKenzie stared sourly at the array of blinking lights, buzzers, and com links in his new office. Never had he longed more for the freedom of open space and the privacy of a small cruiser. Instead he was a prisoner again, confined by his sense of honor and responsibility, by his promises to Kate, by the noisy, demanding, bustling, chaotic, bloody city which sprawled many stories below his windows. Vardalia, beautiful, desperate Vardalia, capital of the Three Systems Alliance.

His glance fell upon a holoimage of the office's former occupant: Prime Minister Pelleas Karlson. MacKenzie glared at the picture.

"You can have this job, Karlson! Have your blessed city and then some." He grabbed up the cube but the image went dark. Cursing, he tossed it to the floor where it flickered dimly, sometimes flashing an eye, a nose. Pieces of Karlson.

A com link line chimed. "Ti-ling to see MacKenzie," announced a high, fluting mechvoice.

"Who? What the hell does she want? How does she know I'm here?" MacKenzie hit the entry key. *No, that was the coffee dispenser. Maybe this one.*

The door flew open.

A beautiful dark-haired woman stood on the threshold staring at him from almond-shaped eyes. She was tiny, no larger than a child, and exquisitely formed. Her skin was golden, her mouth a curved series of red petals. She moved with elaborate self-assurance. Her robes, green silk shot through with metallic threads, were of the finest quality. A fancy woman. Very fancy.

Mac stared. "How did you get that door open?"

"It's easy when you know the secret access code," she said. "I'm Ti-ling." She paused. Obviously she expected him to recognize her name.

MacKenzie stared at her in growing annoyance. He didn't have time to play games. "Is that supposed to impress me for some reason? You're intruding."

She let out an exasperated-sounding sigh and sauntered deeper into the room, hips swinging. Not a child, no. She settled into a webseat with a proprietary air and smiled again. She was good at it. "I had a special relationship with Pelleas Karlson."

"I see. So now you expect me to help you in some way? Lady, I don't care who you were or knew, the damned line forms to the right. Wait your turn."

Ti-ling's smile widened. "I don't think *you* understand me, MacKenzie. The question is, how can I help you?"

"Who said I needed your help?"

"You can't even operate the door in 'your' office."

MacKenzie wrinkled his nose. "You've got me there."

"Here, you push that button, and that one." She leaned over his desk, indicating molded inset panels.

"Thank you. But you didn't come here just to tell me which buttons to push. Are you looking for a job?"

"I just want to be helpful."

Somehow I doubt that that's all you want, Mac thought. "That's very kind of you. However, I'm sure I'll be able to figure things out here on my own." He opened the door. "Now, I really am very busy."

Her smile faded. "I still don't think that you understand all that I'm offering you." Her eyes were as black as space.

"Oh, rest assured that I do, miss. But I think that your style of help went out with Pelleas Karlson. Good day." He turned his back on her and began shifting reports from one screen to another.

When he turned back around, she was gone.

* * *

In a different wing of the Crystal Palace, Merrick the Blackbird was acquainting himself with some of the perks of his new position: aged and marinated smoke sticks. Pelleas Karlson had kept a goodly supply well-sealed and Merrick was quick to liberate one and trigger its self-ignition.

Puffing up a cloud of lavender smoke, he inhaled, sighed, and nodded. A man of rich tastes, Karlson.

A selection of liquors in elaborately faceted decanters lined two curved and fluted shelves. Merrick mulled over his choices. Red? Black? Bright green? He decided to sample a thimbleful of silvery stuff that pooled in odd shapes within its container. The sensation on his tongue was that of frozen violets, followed by a molten surge, with an aftertaste of spice. He nodded as the liquid burned its way down into his stomach, and poured a more generous portion into a carved purple goblet.

Pelleas Karlson's state apartments were a faded shadow of their former glory owing to long neglect as the former Prime Minister's mindsalt addiction took its course. The gemstone walls were in need of polishing, the draperies were cobwebbed and sooty, and most surfaces had a soft sheen from a fine layer of dust.

Merrick told himself that everything could be put to rights by a little spitting and polishing. He sank down onto the velvety cushioned wallseat. Dust spewed upward in clouds.

Coughing, he added dusting to the list of housekeeping chores that needed attending to.

The door chimed, and he palmed the control. A panel slid noisily open; he made a mental note to get it oiled.

On the doorsill stood two former members of Karlson's elite security force. A tall, big-boned blonde woman named Coral Raintree and Robard Fichu, a short, foppish man with slicked-back dark hair and sharp features, had presented themselves at his doorstep.

At the sight of Merrick, they pulled back, recognition dawning in their eyes.

"Raintree, isn't it?" Merrick said, squinting. "Raintree and Fichu. You were part of Karlson's enforcement network. Yeah, I remember. Negotiators." He let out a rasping guffaw. "Which meant that if people didn't agree to what you asked, you'd threaten, you'd warn, and then you'd send in the shock troops. Now what the hell do you want?"

Fichu blanched, but Coral Raintree took a deep breath. *She has guts,* Merrick thought. *Always did.* "An alliance," she said. "We want to discuss an alliance with the new powers of Vardalia."

Merrick's eyebrows arched in surprise. *Interesting,* he thought. These two could be useful. But they seemed too eager and he mistrusted that. "Your former boss left this city in a mess and all the new brooms are busy. Why should I waste time on a partnership with you?"

"We have many interests in common."

Merrick grunted noncommittally.

Raintree frowned. "We can be useful. Surely you can see that for yourself."

"Well, now, there's useful and then there's useful. How do you know what I need, or want?" Merrick asked. He wondered if Lyle MacKenzie had sent these two stooges over as goads, to get him to admit his own plans, to test him. Karlson would have done it. But Mac wasn't that subtle.

"For example," Raintree said, "We know the finest dealers in luxury items on the planet."

"I'm listening."

Fichu tossed a hank of lank hair back out of his eyes and warmed to his work. "Tonnoso liquors, both the green and the exceedingly rare black. Magnificent pearls from the White Sea, prized throughout the Three Systems. Mindstones. Or salt." At this last, the excitement in Fichu's voice was obvious.

Merrick gave him a crooked smile. "I wouldn't touch that salt if you held a disruptor to my right ear, a blowtorch to my left, and kicked me in the ass."

The smaller man blanched, but recovered quickly, laughing too hard and long.

"Well," Raintree said. "What about cloth spun from the belly fur of bambera pups, or priceless artifacts found at the bottom of the Miklos Chasm, or . . ."

A buzzer went off, interrupting her recitation. It took Merrick some little time to locate its source. The viewscreen. He hit a button that he thought might activate the viewer and got a squawk from the com board. He hit another and a series of chimes began to ring. On the next try, he got the master control for the office.

"Can I help you?" inquired a low mechvoice.

"Yeah," Merrick said. "Turn on the viewscreen and turn off all those other damned noisemakers!"

The viewscreen came to life. It spanned one entire wall of the office, and it was suddenly filled with a network of angry faces, all speaking at once.

"Rand Koobin here, machinists' union. We haven't been paid in weeks. No pay, no play, and I don't care who's in charge there. Somebody's got the keys to the money box. Don't tell me different. You want things to work, you get us our credits."

Another face, a thin, bald man, who spoke with a gruff woman's voice: "If you want your lights and heat, you'd better approve the new contract we've sent you. No more of these hardship wages. Karlson is gone. We all get a living wage now."

And another: gray-haired, tough-eyed, in a cook's stained neckpiece. Beside him, a woman with short yellow hair and a slash of a mouth, and next to her, a fat man with a greasy black pompadour.

The com union. The water treatment engineers. The street sweepers. Nobody in Vardalia had been paid in a fortnight and the din of dunning filled the room.

"Computer," Merrick yelled, "tell those complainers to contact Lyle MacKenzie. Better yet, transfer all calls to his office. And kill that sound!"

On screen every mouth moved angrily, but all else was still. A moment later, block by block, the angry faces disappeared and the screen went blank.

Merrick glanced at his visitors and jerked his head toward the now-silent screen. "You heard all that. Demonstrate your usefulness and perhaps then I'll demonstrate my gratitude." He paused. "The labor unions are threatening to strike, testing us. You're trained negotiators, yes? Negotiate with them. Get them settled down. Then we'll talk."

Raintree gave her companion a significant look. The two rose, nodded, and walked swiftly to the door.

Merrick smiled and toasted their departure, raising his purple goblet high. "I might just get to like this job."

* * *

Kayla was in her pressure suit, awaiting the final shove out of the *Antimony*'s belly, a cold birth for her little shuttle. She checked the relays one last time and gave Iger the go-ahead.

"You'll stay in radio contact?" he said.

"I promised, didn't I?"

"If you don't rendezvous with me in twelve hours,

I'm coming down there after you, regardless of what Keller said."

"Iger, we've been through this."

"I don't trust him."

"Do you think I do? But I've got no choice if we want to find Salome, Rab, and Arsobades."

"If they're even still alive. Our scans of the planet sure didn't turn them up."

"Don't talk like that. Don't even think like that. Of course they're alive. And we're going to find them."

There was a brief silence, then Iger said, "Sorry."

"Shuttle launching now." That cut off all further conversation.

She could feel the increase in g's as the acceleration of the shuttle forced her back into her seat. The small pod ship cleared the side of the *Antimony* and was flying free in space under its own power.

Kayla looked down and was startled by the scarred face of Styx filling the viewscreen. It was an angry, intimidating sight: a reddish, mottled, ice-encrusted landscape dotted with extinct volcanoes. And it was getting closer with every beat of her heart.

Home? That was the face of home? That frozen, ugly, forbidding world? No. At least, not in Kayla's memory. When she thought of home at all, she remembered warm, glowing interiors. The translucence of green crystal. The scent of hydroponics. Life. That had nothing to do with the outside of this planet, nothing at all.

She remembered life inside Styx, and what had made her leave it. She bared her teeth in a grimace of anger.

"You'll be sorry, Yates," she said. "Even if I have to crawl through every tunnel in the planet to find you."

She might have said more, but there was a flash of orange light, a shrill beeping, and the shuttle's speed increased.

"Kayla, what's happening?" Iger called.

The face of Styx was getting larger, faster. Too fast.

"Don't know." She pushed buttons, slammed her palm against the keypads. The lights blinked blue-red-orange, but nothing happened.

"Can you fire retros? Slow down?"

"Negative. Controls are frozen."

"Kayla, if you can't slow that shuttle, it'll crash on the surface of Styx."

She couldn't respond. All she could see was the face of her own home world, pink and white, coming up to kill her.

Chapter Three

Kayla stared, transfixed, at the viewscreen. Then the spell broke and she unstrapped herself. Reaching up she grasped one of the ridged wall holds, and pulled herself out of her seat. Hand over hand in the shuttle's light gravity she made her way across the tiny craft to the jet pack and escape-suit stowage. With sure, quick movements she pulled the suit on over her pressure suit, shrugged into the harness of the jet pack, and locked it closed over her shoulders. The power levels showed bright yellow in her visor readout. Full power. The suit's oxygen system hissed air into her lungs.

"Abandoning ship."

"I've got your suit mike locked in," Iger said. "Switch that homing signal on, too."

Kayla triggered the tracking signal and pressed the switch that blew the hatch. Before she had time to think, she was pulled out amidst a cloud of whitish vapor: oxygen.

Silently the shuttle fell away from her, dwindling down toward the surface of Styx and annihilation.

"Reading your signal, Katie," Iger said. "Nice and strong. Can you hear me?"

The universe was whirling and Kayla spun with it.

"Katie, answer me!"

Her stomach was rebelling. Another minute of this and she would surely vomit. Where were the controls for the jet pack?

"Katie, please."

She fired the jet pack and the universe slowed down. Stopped. That was better.

"Iger, I'm all right."

"Thank the gods."

She was a speck, a tiny bit of protoplasmic flotsam against the immensity of an entire planet. Iger's voice was her only link to the human realm. "Keep talking."

Iger's voice shook with his relief. "Just maintain that altitude. I'll bring the *Antimony* in for you."

It was tempting. Stay put and wait for him to come scoop her up. But Styx filled the sky beneath her. She had made a promise. She would keep it.

She took careful aim.

"Katie, you're drifting from my coordinates."

She fired her jets.

"Katie, what are you doing?"

Fired them again.

"Katie! Wait!"

But she was moving too fast to respond, arrowing down and down toward her home, where she had promised to meet her oldest enemy. The cooler packs in her suit repulsed the heat buildup as she flew through Styx's vestigial atmosphere. She felt the planet's gravity grabbing for her.

For a moment vertigo had her and she was certain that she would fall and fall forever, right through her world and out the other side. But another spurt from the jets reminded Kayla that she could control her velocity and her approach. She wouldn't crash and burn. She would come in slowly, find a place to land, and somehow make her way into the planet.

Kayla triggered her radio, hovering. "Iger, I need your help. Get me a reading on the Port doors."

"The what?"

"Styx Port. There were four sets of planet doors through which merchant ships could enter and leave. I can't find them from up here, there's too much ice in the way. You'll have to locate them and beam that telemetry into my jet pack controls."

"Have you lost your mind?"

"I don't have time to argue. Do it."

She hung there, waiting. A moment later his voice crackled across the headphones. "Confirmed. I've found the doors."

"Signal them that I'm approaching and feed them my position."

"Signal who?"

"Styx Port Authority."

"Huh, that's a good one." Iger's tone was especially mordant. "Nobody's home, Katie."

"What?"

"Don't you think I've already tried raising Styx Port? Nada, no response. There's not even any indication that the Port brain is on."

"Wonderful. How the hell am I going to get in there?"

"I might be able to key the doors by relay. If, and it's a big if, I can access the main Styx Port brain system."

Kayla tried to remember where the ops center of Styx Port had been located. A trip to Styx Port with her father years ago came blurrily into focus, and in memory she saw again the busy robot cranes and loaders crawling along the sleek and shiny shuttles, a palleted shipment of mindstones ready to be loaded, a huge space full of flashing lights and machine noises. "Try a meter behind the planet doors. But keep in mind that Styx Port was built long before I was born—the main brain might not speak any of the modern com languages."

"Then how am I supposed to talk to it?"

"See if the *Antimony*'s knowbot has a store of old com speak. Check the back brain."

For long, maddening minutes she heard nothing. Then Iger's voice was back, loud.

"Got it. Running a series of requests now."

"Any response?"

"Nothing happened so far."

The pale face of Styx waited below, maddeningly close and far at the same time. "Keep trying."

"Still no luck."

Just as Kayla was beginning to despair, to think that she would have to relent and allow Iger to reclaim her, she heard him mutter excitedly.

"Iger? What was that?"

"Wait. Just a minute. Think I got something."

Slowly, ponderously, a mouth was opening in the side of the planet. Not a mouth, she reminded herself. Doors. Great slabs of frozen rock were cracking and falling away as long-unused machinery came to life, moving, breaking ice.

A vast space loomed, dark, cavernous.

In there. She had to go in there.

Deep breath. Another one. Now.

Kayla triggered her jet pack and dove through the doors into the dark heart of her planet.

Dark, so dark. Where were the walls? The floor? Kayla turned on her helmet lamp and saw that the space she was in curved steadily downward. She had no choice but to continue downward.

"Iger?"

For answer all she heard was the buzz of static. She had lost him, at least temporarily. She was alone.

Along one wall were grids, ancient tracks for shuttles coming and going, bearing supplies, mindstones, and once, several years ago, a young girl stowaway with no other way off-planet. The memory made her smile briefly.

—Is that how you escaped?

The mindvoice was so loud, so immediate, that Kayla gasped. Where had it come from? She probed around her, then realized that the voice was familiar and had come from inside her head. It belonged to a peculiar interloper, a parasitic mindghost who had latched onto her when she had first used her mind-powers to penetrate the Mindstar. But it was a long time since she had heard its sibilant whispers.

—Golias! You're alive?

—In a manner of speaking. I'm alive in your head, yes. If you call this life.

—Spare me the fine distinctions. I know what you are. But you've been silent for so long, I thought that you had been destroyed when the Mindstar burned out.

—Nearly. It left me, shall we say, comatose. But this excitement has certainly awakened and invigorated me.

—I never thought I'd be so happy to have a mindghost for company.

—Thank you ever so much. Where in the Three Systems have you taken us? And can't you manage to land on a planet like a normal person?

—Styx. My home world.

—Oh, jolly. A more hopeless, godforsaken place would be difficult to imagine. And are we making this trip for sentimental reasons?

—I've got an appointment with an old enemy.

—Better and better.

Briefly, she explained to Golias why she was meeting Yates Keller and what she hoped to achieve.

—Have you used your mindpowers to scan for him here?

—Not yet. Besides, it's tricky in here. The crystalline structures within the caves can bounce probes right back to you. And the false echoes can lead you on—and on. Now be quiet and let me concentrate before I run us into a wall.

The tunnel was widening, the slope becoming less pronounced. And suddenly, she was in a vast cavern. Her headlamp revealed actual floor, and she shut down her jet pack to place her feet gently upon solid rock.

Lights came on around her, brilliant, blinding. For long moments she could see little but flashing shapes until her eyes grew accustomed to the glare.

A huge room, the ceiling disappearing in the radiance of the lights high above her head. Hulking mechs and cargo containers lined the loading docks. Lines and grapples hung like so many silvery vines above the ramps and accessways. Necessary, all of it, the bones and sinews of a major port, but all of it silent, dead. Styx Port was a ghost port.

She was in a shuttle bay. Two old ships sat gathering dust, long idle in their berths. The other berths were empty. Her steps echoed loudly upon the flooring plates.

Home.

—*Where are we?* Golias asked.

—*Part of Styx Port. A shuttle bay. We must have triggered a lighting system.*

—*Are there many people here?*

—*I don't think there's anybody here at all.*

—*What happened to them?*

—*Your guess. I'm not very familiar with the area around the Port. Once we get closer to my family's stake, I'll recognize things. I hope.*

Kayla left the shuttle bay and walked along an empty, well-lit corridor. Somewhere she heard the low hum of machinery, almost a sensation rather than a sound. Perhaps she could find the Port Ops Center and use the com board there to contact Iger.

But the corridor led her to another hall, and another. The sound of machinery faded and was gone.

—*I'm not sure where we are. Maybe I should try to find my family's old district and then contact Iger.*

—*Why don't you take a probe for this Keller person? It might be useful to know where he is.*

Kayla decided that Golias was probably right: better to pinpoint Keller's location than to let him surprise her.

She took a deep breath and opened her mind, searching for Yates Keller's mind signature.

At first she perceived nothing more than dim echoes impossible to trace, the remnants of the thoughts of people who had passed through here. The crystalline walls functioned as an unreliable echo chamber: Cyrilite could amplify thought fragments and shadows, or completely muffle them.

She tried a narrow probe, snaking it along the halls and tunnels. Every now and then she was certain that she had come close to fixing upon an active mind, but as she intensified the probe's focus, the source of the stimulus would disappear.

It was slow, maddening work. For a second, a mere heartbeat, she felt what she was certain was Yates Keller's mind. But that moved and was gone before she could do more than achieve a vague reading on his location. Had it even been Yates? Had it really been anyone at all?

She scanned her surroundings. She was in an unfamiliar district far from her parents' house, a neighborhood of small dwellings carved from the living rock. Each cave was dark, each door barred, with no sign of current habitation.

Where is everybody? she wondered.

She passed into a quarter where house after house seemed to be occupied by mechs. Some blinked blue lights as they sorted ore along winding conveyor belts. Others were dark and silent. What little mining activity there was appeared to be completely mechanized. Styx was inhabited by mechs and ghosts.

Now she passed a more familiar landmark: the

clinic where she had been treated after the cave-in that killed her parents. She touched the translucent green wall of the old structure. It was empty now, she could sense that. What had happened to Doctor Ashley? What had happened to all the miners?

And here, here was the warren of rooms that had functioned as a school for the miners' children. Kayla remembered spending many a long afternoon here, swinging her heels against the stone benches and listening to the crystalline tinkle of stone chips flaking off under the assault of her bootheels.

She spurred herself past it and reluctantly made for her parents' house.

It was a ruin, the door gone, the insides ransacked. Nothing remained of what she had remembered. Whether from spite or out of neglect, her family home had become a debris-filled cave, dark and malodorous. Home.

Swearing, Kayla pulled back and closed her eyes. She could see it as it had been. The bambera-skin rug, the pictures, the hydroponics. But that was then and this was now. For a moment she wanted to smash and destroy everything in sight, to wreck the mining mechs. But no, that was foolish. She was there for one reason only, to save her friends. Shrines to her past were a foolish waste of time, and she shouldn't have expected any better than the decay that she had found.

The next dwelling had obviously functioned as an

ops center and was filled with boards and screens. Kayla thought she recognized a com board in the corner and reached toward the palm pad to key it on.

—Wait! Do you want to announce your arrival?

—To whom, Golias? There's nobody here. I've got to notify Iger that I'm all right before he comes blasting in here after me.

—You'll be inviting attention, and trouble.

—That's my decision, isn't it?

The board came to life beneath her hands, lights winking gently, blue-red, blue-green.

"Iger," she said. "Can you hear me? Iger, come in."

No answer.

She counted off several minutes and tried again. "Iger, this is Katie. I'm all right. I made it. Please respond. Iger, can you hear me?"

Faintly, through gusts of static, over the great distance, a voice spoke. A blessedly familiar voice. "Katie? Katie, send again. Katie, I lost the last part of your message."

"Iger!" The relief made her laugh. "I'm here, in Styx. I'm all right. Do you hear me?"

"Affirmative." She could hear the smile in her voice. "Gods, Katie, you gave me a scare. It's been hours. I thought Keller had ambushed you."

"Not likely. There's no sign of him here."

"I don't understand."

"Neither do I."

"Do you want me to land?"

"Negative. I'll make radio contact again in twelve hours. Do you hear me?"

"Affirmative. Twelve hours, Katie, or I'll come looking for you."

"Iger, promise me you won't do that."

"But—"

"Iger, you can't put Third Child at risk like that. Promise me. If I don't manage to contact you in twelve hours, wait as long as you think makes sense, then head back to Vardalia."

"Katie—"

"Out." She shut down the connection and went to look for Yates Keller.

He had promised to meet her, blackmailed her into this trip. But the bastard wasn't there.

She checked the old Keller homestead. It was a black ruin like her own home.

She looked in the Guild Hall. It was filled with deactivated mining mechs, stacked one against the other.

Where is he? she wondered. And, uneasy, she began to wish she had warned Iger to keep his shields up.

There, out of the corner of her eye, a flash of movement. A person? She turned to look.

Gone.

"Wait!" She sent a probe after the fleeing figure but it bounced off a wall and came back to her.

Angry, she pursued as best she could, but the figure had vanished completely.

She was back among the blinking mechs in their caves. And she knew then, with heart-stopping finality, that Yates Keller would not meet her, that this was just part of his cat-and-mouse game. He had lured her back to Styx for some twisted reason.

—*What now?* Golias asked.

—*I'm going to do a little research.*

The brainboard came to life under her hands. She scanned for the most recent entries on "Styx, inhabitants" and found a tape of Pelleas Karlson congratulating all the residents of Styx as they embarked upon their brave new lives elsewhere.

Karlson had emptied out her world and sent in mechs to carve anything of value out of the cave walls.

So the place was empty. She had probably just imagined sensing other human beings.

Kayla was about to shut down the board when a very recent entry caught her attention: a report filed by a serving engineer, dated a few months ago.

A round, pink face, pale blue eyes, slightly hyperthyroid, stared out at her and said, "There's somebody here, somebody in the tunnels. A woman, a ghostly presence. I saw her in the deeper tunnels, just a flash, a pale face receding into the dark. Thin, blonde, with a sad face and pale green eyes."

The transmission ended, but Kayla didn't notice.

The man had just described her mother, Teresa Reed.

Chapter Four

Lyle MacKenzie watched the lights of Vardalia come on below him, yellow jewels twinkling in the lavender gloom of dusk. He took a sip from the glass of rum on the desk. His desk, now.

A pretty sight, Vardalia, with all of her lanterns lit. And from this altitude you could sit back, admire the glow, and never notice how much trouble she was in. She deserved better, did poor beleagured Vardalia.

Today, alone, he had quelled a rebellion by the major banks. With the end of Pelleas Karlson's reign, all city loans were being called in. But the Treasury appeared to be empty. Where was the money? How was anything going to be paid for? City employees were demanding their pay. The garbage collectors were threatening to strike.

MacKenzie rubbed his head. He had never asked for this job. It was the last thing he had ever wanted. But he would, by damn, make a go of it, do a better job than Karlson had. He would stick by this city, clean it up, and make it run. He raised his glass to Vardalia. "You and me," he said, and took a healthy sip.

His gaze rose up above the purpling towers and into the night sky. Xenobe had not yet risen and he could see the stars, faint pinpricks of white in the gloom. Where was Katie right now? Had she landed on Styx yet? he wondered. When would she return? Was she in trouble?

He sighed, told himself that there was nothing he could do about it.

The office main access buzzer went off. Who the hell wanted in at this hour?

"Come."

"Hello, Mac. It's been a long time."

MacKenzie stared across the long office at his visitor and gaped in disbelief. It took him a moment to find his voice.

"I never thought I'd see you again," he said quietly. "I thought you were dead. What in the nine hells of Denebia are you doing here?"

"Is that any way to greet me?"

"Cristobal, you don't want to hear any other greeting I'd care to give you."

Cristobal stared at him angrily from dark eyes sheltered by lids with an epicanthic fold. His glossy black hair fell halfway to his shoulders, and his green stretchsuit had seen hard use.

MacKenzie glared back at him.

There had never been any great warmth between the two men, and their last contacts had been filled with hatred. MacKenzie was shaken to see a man he had taken for dead—a man who had blatantly betrayed him and the rest of the War Minstrels—standing in front of him, smiling an ingratiating smile.

"How the hell did you survive the firestorm when we shot up the Alliance's fleet?" MacKenzie demanded. "I thought you were killed when Katie took out St. Ilban's orbitals."

"I knew it was a suicide run," Cristobal said. "I pulled out of orbit and made for Liage. Stayed there until the dust settled." He gave the office a quick, approving glance. "Very nice place. You've done well for yourself, Mac. And where's Katie?"

"Away on business."

"A pity. I wanted to see her."

"I doubt that she wants to see you." MacKenzie waited, hoping to get a volatile reaction to his dig.

"Too bad." Cristobal shrugged. "Guess I'll have to deal with you, then."

"Why did you come back?"

A look of irritation crossed the smooth face. "I thought you might be able to use my help."

"Or did you think you might be able to use mine?"

The two men glared at one another.

"You haven't changed, Mac."

"Neither have you," MacKenzie snapped. "Always

looking for the main chance, aren't you? But your problem is that you want whoever you use to love you, too. Forget it. Somebody in my family already paid the price for loving you."

Cristobal looked down and away from him. "You never forget, Mac, do you?"

"Or forgive."

"You know that people here are happy to see me," Cristobal said. "Word's getting around that I'm back. They remember that I helped liberate them, and they wouldn't like hearing that you had shoved me aside for your own glory. I was there on that prison ship with them. Not you."

MacKenzie knew he should be outraged, should feel something other than dull irritation at Cristobal's threats. But he had come too far, had done too much to have spare energy for anger. He expelled his breath in a long sigh and sat down heavily. "What do you want?"

Cristobal sat opposite him and leaned in close. "To be part of things."

"You want a job?"

Cristobal coughed delicately into his hand. "A job isn't exactly what I had in mind."

"No?" MacKenzie showed his teeth in a feral smile. "What, then?"

"A power-sharing."

MacKenzie fought down an urge to laugh. Was

there no limit to the man's ambition? "You'd like to be in charge again, is that it?"

Cristobal nodded.

The nerve of the man! "I'll see what I can do." MacKenzie swung away to stare at the city map engraved upon one wall. He pretended to ponder it, wondering all the while if he should press the security buzzer beneath the desk. Cristobal could be bundled away into one of the dungeons beneath the Crystal Palace. It was tempting. The Minister of Police, Darius Peters, had been tremendously cooperative. But if word ever got out, Cristobal's followers would cause trouble. No, it was best to give him at least a semblance of what he'd asked for, and make it seem desirable.

"What about Minister of Sewage?" MacKenzie offered. "Should think that'd be a job you could relate to."

Cristobal gave him a dark look.

"No? Then what about the utilities? I need somebody to manage those. Merrick pretends to, but he's so busy lining his goddamned pockets and stealing everything that isn't nailed down that he can't be bothered with keeping the lights on."

"Not exactly in my line."

MacKenzie nodded and sprang the trap. "Well, what about running the Western District of Vardalia? I need somebody over there. I'll even arrange for transport."

Cristobal's smile flashed. "I knew you'd see reason, old friend. Together we'll turn this place around." He held out his hand.

MacKenzie ignored the outstretched palm, leaned back, and crossed his arms across his chest. "Don't be so quick to exult, Cris. Not until you see the Western District."

"What do you mean?"

"It's mostly landfill, with light industry, and a few squatters too poor even to roam the streets of more prosperous neighborhoods. That's your kingdom, Cris. You can preside over the mechs and seabirds, boss around the beggars." He paused, smiling in earnest at Cristobal's mounting anger. But his grin faded as he said, "Take it or leave it. But keep in mind that this is all that you'll ever get from me. One offer. This one."

"And if I refuse?"

"That's all right with me, too. But this is the only favor you get. Don't be too hasty in refusing it."

"All right, Mac. I suppose I owe you one."

"Yes," MacKenzie said coldly. "Yes, you do." Again they locked gazes. "Be here tomorrow at nine and I'll have someone take you to your new office."

The next morning, MacKenzie was amused and not in the least surprised when the escort he had provided reported that Cristobal had briefly toured the Western District, had taken one look at the warehouse that was his "office," and had angrily ordered the party to return him to Vardalia proper.

Stay away from me, Cristobal, MacKenzie thought. *That's the best advice I can give you.*

* * *

When Merrick the Blackbird answered the door of his apartment, he expected to see another merchant in the endless stream of sellers of pilfered merchandise.

Word had gone out that the Blackbird didn't care how the inventory had been acquired, he merely wanted to be shown the best of it, and the dealers of Vardalia had flocked to his office. The last dealer had made the mistake of thinking he could palm off third-rate cutlery and fourth-rate gems. Merrick had given him the boot, literally.

But the man waiting outside his door now wasn't a merchant. At least, not a merchant in hard goods.

"Cristobal," Merrick said smoothly. "Haven't seen you around these parts. Back from the dead, or just gone vampire?"

Cristobal made a good attempt at a smile, but Merrick could see that something had gotten him riled.

"Come in and make yourself comfortable. Smoke sticks? Telafian brandy?"

"Thanks. You're certainly more hospitable than Mac was."

"So you've already been to see Mac, have you?" Merrick filed that away for later investigation. Cristobal wanted something, that was obvious. What would it bring Merrick in return? He waited until Cristobal had finished a generous glass of brandy and at least two smoke sticks before getting down to business.

"So, Cris. I should tell you that I never expected to see you alive again. Especially after that shitty little maneuver you pulled on us."

"If Katie had had her way, you wouldn't have."

So he's blaming Katie, is he? Merrick thought. *Might as well go along with it and see where he leads.*

"She did, did she?"

"Sure. She wanted me dead and gone so she could rule without any obstacles. But I knew that my supporters, my people, would never accept that. So I pretended to do what she wanted and, instead, waited, hiding."

"A wise move."

Cristobal, obviously gaining confidence that he had a sympathetic listener, flashed a real smile. Merrick encouraged him, poured him another glass of brandy, nodded, and listened.

And, as the old bounty hunter had hoped, Cristobal relaxed and grew expansive under the warmth of the brandy and attention.

"A necessary move," he said. "I knew my time

would come. I came back here hoping to find Katie, to settle things with her."

Merrick watched his visitor bemusedly. He was crazy, was old Cristobal. Of course, that didn't mean he couldn't be useful. Gently, he directed him back toward his own interests. "What happened with MacKenzie?"

"He doesn't realize how much he owes to me. He tried to give me some third-rate job in the backwaters here, as if I'd be satisfied with that while he hogged all the glory."

"Obviously, he was wrong."

"He'll find out."

"Will he?"

"Oh, he'll overstep himself. Outsmart himself."

"And it would be best if wiser folk were ready to pick up the pieces, yes?"

Cristobal met his gaze, eyes blazing. "I'm glad you understand me so well."

"Let's drink to our understanding."

"You wouldn't, uh, have any mindsalt around, would you?" The casual tone of the query didn't quite match the eager look Cristobal's eyes.

Mindsalt? Merrick filed that away for later use, too. "Sorry. Never touch the stuff." He refilled Cristobal's goblet. "Have to make do with good brandy. Drink up, man."

Merrick waited until most of that glass had been

absorbed before he began probing again. "I was wondering if you could clear something up for me, Cris."

"Name it."

"Brayton's Rock."

Cristobal sighed, threw back the last of the brandy, and set the glass down with a loud clink. "Bad business, that."

"What the hell happened? Who blew it?"

"Yates Keller."

"Himself?"

"Oh, no, never. He wouldn't get his hands that dirty. But he was convinced that the Free Trade revolutionaries had a foothold on Brayton's Rock. He couldn't clear them out with his security forces, so he decided the place had to go."

"But blowing it up? With N-ware?"

"Yes."

Merrick repressed a shudder. "How did he find it? I thought that stuff wasn't being made anymore."

Suddenly Cristobal was transfixed by some microscopic speck on the floor. It had his full attention. "Umm, there was a cache of the stuff around in Vardalia."

"Even so. Surely he had other, cleaner, weapons, just as effective."

"He wanted it to look like the rebels had done it themselves, a terrorist raid gone wrong, blowing themselves up. He figured that the old N-ware would be traced to them."

"And who put him on to the N-ware?"

"I don't know."

Merrick was certain that Cristobal was lying to him, but he gave no sign of it. He had the information that he'd wanted. And he had had a few friends on Brayton's Rock who had died in that blast. Good friends.

"I think you should take the job that MacKenzie gave you," he said.

"What?" Cristobal looked up, startled. "Heven't you been listening to anything I've said?"

"I've listened to everything. And I think you should take it. Your best chance."

"No!"

"Use your head, man. We have to wait. Bide our time. So stay in place and watch."

Light dawned in Cristobal's eyes and he nodded.

Good, Merrick thought. At least that much had gotten through to him.

He bid Cristobal farewell, closed the door, and shook his head. He had another player in place. Sooner or later he would figure out what to do with him.

Chapter Five

Kayla crept along the tunnels of Styx, crunching crystals underfoot, making odd musical notes with every step she took. The tunnels were barely lit: half the glowglobes had malfunctioned—when was the last time they had been serviced? She moved slowly through the green shadows, moving from pool of light to pool of light.

Home, and yet not home. Nothing felt remotely familiar. She could have been walking within a tunnel on any of a thousand worlds. The more she reached for a sense of connection, of meaning, the more it seemed to elude her.

She walked alone, cracking crystals beneath her feet, with only a mindghost for company.

—At least you're here, Golias.

—More or less.

What she had was a mind full of suspicion, all of it trained upon Yates Keller. Where was that bastard? Why had he lured her here if he wasn't going to meet her? Was he planning to trigger another explosion like the one that had killed her parents and finish her, too?

She scanned for Keller's mind signature, but the crystalline walls made a mockery of her attempts, fragmenting her probes, bouncing them back at her.

A mind full of suspicion . . . and a rapidly growing obsession. The description of the woman who had been seen by the engineer: could it have been her mother? Was it possible that Teresa Reed had survived the explosion that had killed her husband?

Kayla told herself she was crazy to even entertain such a thought. But she desperately wanted to believe, to hope, just the same. Was her mother still alive, wandering lost and confused through the lower tunnels? Had she been alive and wandering for all these years?

What if? she thought. *What if, what if, what if?*

Despite the implausibility of the theory, Kayla felt hope igniting within her, and she was both angered and excited by it, frightened and exhilarated.

The mindghost stirred within her. *—Kayla, you don't really believe this. How could it be? You told me that your mother died years ago.*

—I don't know, Golias.

—It's a coincidence. Or a fantasy. You said yourself that there's nobody living here.

—But I don't know that for certain. I've sensed something, heard other minds.

—Those might have been echoes of previous residents, caught in these walls. You have no proof.

His pessimism began to annoy her. *—I don't have to. If there's a chance, just a chance, I've got to find out.*

—What about your missing friends?

—Golias, we're talking about my mother!

The mindghost made no reply.

—Golias?

Silence met her probe.

Good, Kayla thought. *One less distraction to worry about.*

She began scanning in earnest now, searching for her mother's specific mind signature.

The readings she took were inconclusive, odd, but she kept at it, casting her mindprobes ahead and around her.

What was that?

A flicker. A hint of a thought, and familiar.

She pursued it, following a path that led deeper and deeper into the mines.

Wait, she thought. *Please wait. I'm coming. Don't run away from me.*

The trail was a maddening glimmer in the corner of her mind. Following it, she roamed deeper and deeper, into a district that she had never seen before, through wide mech-carved tunnels that had recently been cut.

If Pelleas Karlson had wanted to hollow the planet

out, he had nearly succeeded. Could a man eat a planet?

Echoes resounded, but not of Kayla's making. Footsteps sounded in a nearby corridor, growing louder.

Kayla froze. "Who's there?"

The footsteps ceased.

Cautiously Kayla went forward.

The footsteps started up again.

She moved faster, at a near run. Suspicions roiled through her. Was this some sort of trap set by Yates Keller? She began to regret her rashness, coming here alone, unarmed.

There's always the jet pack, she thought. For emergencies. It would require quite an emergency for her to unleash the pack's immense power. And likely cause a cave-in.

Best to back off and hide. Get a look at whoever her pursuers were.

She rounded a corner, slid into a convenient niche shielded by a spiky stalagmite, and held still.

If they were Yates Keller's people, did that mean that they had taken her mother, too? She shoved the thought down, out of sight, and concentrated on the sounds.

She heard a loud scrabbling nearby and held her breath. Another moment and her pursuer should be visible . . .

A sudden radiance enveloped her, a sound which

became a white numbing aura. Kayla barely had time to register the sensation, to realize that somebody behind her had stunned her with a disruptor, before she flel down into darkness.

* * *

An unfamiliar face was looking at her, floating at right angles to Kayla's perspective.

It took her a moment to realize that she was the one at an odd angle: lying flat, being looking down upon by a thin, pale man with a stern, thin-lipped face and eyes the color of deep space. His hair was obscured by an odd, cowllike hood, deep green, joined to a cloak that fell in velvety folds to the floor.

"Who are you?" she said.

—Natan is my name.

"Why did you chase me?"

—You were treading on holy ground.

His lips never moved, yet his voice was distinct, a high baritone. Mindspeech.

Instinctively Kayla responded in kind. *—You're an empath!*

The man's eyes widened. For a moment he didn't respond, obviously surprised. *—As, apparently, you are.*

—I didn't think there were any of us left here.

—A few remained. And others came to join us.

—Please, can you tell me, is there a woman named Teresa Reed among you? Tall? Blonde, with gray eyes?

Natan didn't answer. Rather, he looked away as though pondering his response.

—Please, is she here? I have to know.

—We never reveal our members to outsiders. We are Charon's Eyes, the guardians of this place. If you join us, you'll come to know who is and is not among us.

—Join you? What do you do?

—We prevent the further exploitation of the holy body of this world. We attempt to heal its wounds.

—Are all of you empaths?

—I won't answer that question. Will you join us?

—I don't know. I don't understand.

—We must learn if you've been sent against us. You came alone, but you bear the signs of the exploiters. You use their tools. And yet you're an empath. It's very curious. But we'll find out.

—But . . .

Kayla faltered and found herself unable to continue, frozen against her will by some potent force not unlike the power of a groupmind. She saw now that she was suspended at the nexus of many minds, mute, incapable of protest as they scanned her. Kayla floated in a clear and soundless space, transfixed by four beams of streaming golden light. Things floated around her, spectral images by turn huge and small, familiar figures with averted faces.

A crying woman whose tears turned to webbed-toe creatures with giant orange eyes. The tears fell in such abundance that a flood of these creatures surrounded her, forming themselves into pyramids that slowly enclosed the woman, obscuring her from sight.

A collapsing sack of flesh from which a weeping skeleton stepped forth, a skeleton cut from living rock, faceted, bold and glowing with malevolent energies.

A cabinet that capered and danced on legs that ended in cloven hooves. From its partly open recesses spilled the severed heads and hearts of an army.

An old woman from whose flesh flowers sprouted and were consumed by fire. They sprouted again and their petals stretched, became arms reaching, grasping glowing gems, blue-red-bronze, became eyes, weeping.

—*What are these images?* Kayla demanded.

Natan's mindvoice, oddly amplified, reverberated all around her.

—*These are the equivalences of your crimes and desires. Your actions. Your life.*

—*That's absurd. You're manufacturing these illusions to try to frighten me.*

—*Your way is paved in blood. You've killed and killed. You think that you're part of the cure, but you carry the illness within you and spread it. You're a carrier, Sister Blood. A vector of the plague of so-called civilization.*

—No, you're wrong. You're crazy.

—You wish to become a martyr, but you fool yourself as to what your cause is. Your cause is death.

—I seek vengeance.

—You seek death.

Throughout this inquisition, the mindghost Golias had been mute. Now he emerged from hiding to engage Kayla's tormentors directly.

—Who are you to judge her? What has she done to you? You see only what you wish to see, interpret only what suits you. Fools! She no more seeks death than I did!

There was a hushed mutter, as of many different minds engaged, conferring. Over it, Natan thundered: *—What is this? Who is that? Another speaks from your mind.*

—Golias, a mindghost.

—How is this possible?

—More things are possible than you can imagine.

—Never have we encountered such.

—Your experiences don't define my existence.

—You are evil.

—Perhaps. But you're crazy.

—When Pelleas Karlson first imported his evil here, we hid in the darkest caverns. We waited until the ships and men bearing the machines had gone, and then we crept out to destroy the evil, to stop its spread. This ground is holy.

—You worship the stones? The mindstones?

—Holy.

—They're only rock. They aren't supernatural, aren't alive.

—We're aware of their inanimate nature. But they are powerful, pure. And when left in place they are harmless. But they cause evil throughout the galaxy. To stop this, the stones must remain here.

—But I agree with you. You want me to join you?

—You only say that to lull us.

—You don't understand.

—Sister Blood, you have been scanned and found wanting. We won't allow you to infect us with your evil.

—You say that you came from here. So did I. Perhaps you knew my parents.

—We're not interested in you or your lineage. What came before is over. All that matters now are the mines, and the halt of the evil, its spread.

Kayla struggled against the mental fetters and felt Golias urging her on, trying to lend her strength.

—You . . . don't . . . understand! Pelleas Karlson is dead. the mining will stop. I didn't come here to expand it or report on you.

—Liar!

—I didn't even know of your existence. Surely you can scan my mind and see that that much, at least, is true.

The light shifted from gold to deep violet. The nightmarish figures vanished.

Green-cowled faces emerged from the shadows, the members of Charon's Eyes, of the groupmind, arrayed around her in a circle. All of them wore the odd habit that Natan had worn. There were men and women of differing ages, races, sizes. Not one of them did Kayla recognize.

They began to spin around her, to orbit as though they were moons, or perhaps planets, and she was the sun.

It's a trick, she thought. *A trick.* But she felt her stomach writhe as the speed of the dizzying orbits increased.

—You claim you want justice, nothing more.

—For the death of my parents, yes.

—Yet you have admitted of being the creator and leader of a great killing force.

—I hated the killing!

—Then why did you allow it?

—I couldn't control everything.

—But you said yourself that you've set this thing in motion.

—It's changed. Gotten bigger, huge, a juggernaut. I don't run it.

—Does it run you?

—No. Yes . . . I don't know.

—How are you different from Karlson?

—He was mad with ambition. No limits to what he hoped to do. We're not like that.

—No? How do you know?

Image of a serpent encircling St. Ilban, a human/ serpent face . . . her face? Pelleas Karlson's. Its visage blurred, shifted, forming different, familiar features, composite faces. A monster of humanity. It stretched across space and reached for Styx, mouth open, teeth sharp and ready.

Golias' mindvoice was an anchor in the maelstrom. —*Steady, Kayla. They're starting to unhinge you.*

—*No, I'm all right.*

—*Remember, you were wondering about the possibility that your mother survived and is among them.*

—*I don't see her here. Surely she would have stopped this as soon as she saw me. She would know me.*

—*Perhaps she's elsewhere.*

—*Then you think there's a chance?*

—*I think that whatever keeps you from losing your focus is of value.*

Natan's mindvoice cut in. —*Silence! You've been judged. Sentence will be carried out.*

Before Kayla could react, she felt the power of the groupmind smiting her, knocking her out of the world one more time.

Chapter Six

Lyle MacKenzie, Merrick the Blackbird, and Cristobal stood before the sea of upturned faces in the grand square of Vardalia. Some were familiar, those of colleagues and rebels. Others were Vardalian merchants, laborers, and officials of the former regime. And many of them, too many, possessed political aspirations of their own.

But regardless of former affiliations, every face looked cold, hostile, suspicious, or downright angry.

MacKenzie stared down at them from his perch upon the temporary stage and again felt misgivings at having accepted the role that Katie had thrust upon him.

War, he thought, *is an easier business to manage than peace. At least in war you know who your enemies are.*

He gave Merrick and Cristobal a sidelong glance, and mused again upon the theme of enemies. In war they weren't often standing next to you, pretending friendship.

Merrick the Blackbird, hulking, dark, crowlike in his black cape, was rumbling at the crowd, something about, "Keeping the lights on, shipments flowing, business as usual."

Business as usual, MacKenzie thought, and repressed a dry chuckle. That was certainly Merrick's motto. He was doing business with both hands, amassing wealth, stockpiling mindstones, moving to control the merchants who controlled the luxury items in Vardalia, and through them trade throughout the scattered remnants of the Three Systems.

And Cristobal, who had belatedly reaccepted MacKenzie's offer of a job, stood there now, wearing expensive embroidered leathers, a mindstone dangling from his ear, and his best angelic expression. How like him to show up when the fighting was over, to demand "his" share of the city. His prize. His. His. His.

Quite a prize, Vardalia. A city that was threatening to come apart like a vivisected body, dividing into political and military factions. The old-style Karlsonites, anxious to grab power. The War Minstrels, as interested in plunder as they were in managing the city they had won. The Ayrists, opposed to all forms of government. The Satamans, opposed to all forms of freedom. Not to mention the labor unions and churches, all clamoring for attention, power, credits, their piece of Vardalia. And the mindsalt addicts, in every group, on every level. Yes, Vardalia was certainly a plum.

MacKenzie was tempted to just let it go. What did he care for politics, for factions, for, in fact, the entire bleeding city of Vardalia? Let it slide into a slime pit and disappear off the face of the universe. Let it sink under the accumulated weight of a hundred thousand bodies, their minds ruined by mindsalt.

Katie had asked him to hold things together.

Katie be hanged, he thought. But he had given his word to her, hadn't he? She had saved his life. He owed her, and when Lyle MacKenzie gave his word, he by-the-gods kept it.

The sound of Katie's name jerked him out of his reverie and back to the assembly.

"And Kate Shadow, what's she done for you lately?"

It was Cristobal, making the point to the crowd that Katie was gone, had, in fact, disappeared without a by-your-leave. Boos and hisses greeted the news.

"Yes, where is she?" Cristobal said. "When there's real work to be done, Kate Shadow has better things to do."

Amidst derisive whistling and clapping, Cristobal warmed to his work. "She may have deserted you, but your real friends and colleagues haven't gone. No! We're right here with you, shoulder to shoulder, in the same mess. The kind of mess that Pelleas Karlson and Kate Shadow left us in."

Before Cristobal could do more damage, MacKenzie shoved him aside, nearly knocking him down. Ignoring his angry look, MacKenzie took his place at the podium.

"Friends," he said. "We're pulling this cart together, and Kate Shadow pulls it alongside us."

The jeering began again.

MacKenzie held up his hand. "Listen to me! Katie was no friend to Karlson. At the risk of her own life she freed you from him. Yes, she's gone, it's true. Gone on urgent business, personal business. And hasn't she earned that right? But she'll be back soon. While she's gone, let's keep things moving, prove that there's life after Pelleas Karlson. Or was he really the only thing that kept Vardalia together?"

A few people cheered but others hissed, some booed, and a few walked away, obviously disgusted.

MacKenzie didn't blame them. He wished that he could walk away too.

"You're an idiot," Merrick the Blackbird said, sotto voce. "Either intimidate them or make love to them. Don't you know anything about crowd control?"

"That never was his strong suit," Cristobal said. He and the Blackbird exchanged quick, amused glances.

MacKenzie watched them, reading the threat to

him in their congruent body language. In a brief shattering moment he saw all there was to see.

So, he thought. *So. So. So. That's how it is. The two of you, and who else? There must be others. I should have expected it. Should have known as soon as Cristobal showed up that he would try to undermine whatever I did, that he would seek out Merrick. And what does the Blackbird owe me? Nothing. Absolutely nothing.*

The gathering dissolved in rancor, the audience hissing and shouting out threats. MacKenzie knew that there was more trouble ahead.

Darius Peters, Minister of Police, stood squarely in his path, blocking him. A dark-skinned man with graying hair and deep-set eyes.

"Peters."

"We should talk, MacKenzie. You can't let this go any further. You've got to institute order. Things are falling apart."

"What did you have in mind, martial law?"

"I don't like it, but I don't see that you've really got a choice here."

MacKenzie shot him a suspicious glance, but Peters looked and sounded sincere.

MacKenzie sized him up. Peters had never given him any trouble, and that in itself was a recommendation.

"I'm serious, MacKenzie."

"I know. And you're right. This was a circus.

We're barely holding on, barely keeping things together."

Peters gave him a thin-lipped smile. "That's the problem with revolutions. What do you do on the morning after?" He beckoned. "Come with me."

The streets they passed through were strewn with garbage, bread rinds, scraps of clothing, cracked holo visors, and indecipherable urban debris.

People sat on the curbside, glassy-eyed, silent. Some had their palms out for charity. Others had given up. Two men were dismantling a deactivated mech by kicking it. A small girl was scraping the side of a building with a jagged piece of ceramsteel.

"Is this the Beggars' Quarter?" MacKenzie asked.

Peters' lips curled. "It's like this in every Quarter, now," he said sourly. His wave encompassed all that they had passed. "That's why I wanted you to see this. This city was once was a paradise. Look at it now. Look at it."

"You miss Karlson?" MacKenzie said acidly. "Want your Prime Minister back, or somebody like him?"

"At least he kept order."

"For a time. Until the mindstones—and salt—got hold of him."

"I can show you my new files," Peters said. "Robberies and burglaries are happening so fast now that my officers can't keep up with them. The perpetrators are mainly the people that you brought in with you."

MacKenzie nodded grimly. So the War Minstrels were reverting to their old ways.

"I've heard tell that most of them were prisoners."

"Some."

"Mac, what have you brought us?"

MacKenzie couldn't resist the black joke. "Your deliverance, Peters. Can't you see it?"

"Well, your blessings are raining down now, fast and furious. It doesn't help that your leader, what's-her-name . . ."

"Kate N. Shadow."

". . . Kate Shadow, that she's gone. These people of yours act like mommy's away and everything is fair game."

MacKenzie chuckled and patted him on the shoulder. "You're a good man, Peters, and you're right. Come see me and we'll talk about what we can do."

The Police Minister's eyes never left his. "Why don't you come see me? At least that way we can be certain of security."

"Good point." The offer was suddenly quite appealing. An ally. MacKenzie could use one. "What about tomorrow morning?"

"Fine. I'll be there." He held out his hand.

MacKenzie grasped it. "Got to get back to work."

They parted, Peters moving away toward Police Headquarters. MacKenzie made his way gloomily toward the Crystal Palace, listening to the curses and cries of Vardalia's citizens, the sounds of breaking glass and howling sirens. His Vardalia.

He had looked forward to a quiet period at his desk, settling the latest series of complaints from the unions, followed by a good, long drink. But Ti-ling was waiting for him in his office. Lovely Ti-ling, Pelleas Karlson's former mistress. Almond-eyed, dark-haired, fine-boned, and as ambitious as she was beautiful. She was wearing a long flowing cloak the color of an emerald's heart. It suited her.

Ti-ling's face lit with a smile. "There you are, Mac. I've been waiting."

"Ti-ling, did we have an appointment?"

She gave him a playful look. "Do I need an appointment?"

"Well, yes, actually." He ignored her pout. "I'm pretty busy. Can this wait?"

"It'll only take a minute."

"I'll time you."

Again the pout. "Mac, I'm not accustomed to being rushed."

"It's a brave new world, Ti-ling. A brave new city. You've got thirty seconds left."

"It's about mindstones."

"Not interested."

"Mac! You haven't heard what I have to offer."

"Whatever it is . . ."

"Did you know that I have the deeds to Pelly's mindstone holdings on Styx."

"Good for you. Enjoy them."

"But *we* could enjoy them. Together. As soon as you get the mines activated again."

"I see." MacKenzie almost smiled. At least he had been right about something this morning. Activate the mines again? Ye gods! "Not asking for very much, are you?"

"Mac." She climbed out of her chair, came over to him, and wound her arms around his neck. Her nails glittered like faceted golden gems. "This would be for us."

He caught her wrists and forced her arms open, freeing himself. "That's a lovely thought, Ti-ling. Don't imagine I'm not flattered. But my answer is still no. No mindstones. No mines on Styx. I don't have time to be anybody's sugar daddy. This city is falling down around our ears because your 'Pelly' got so busy with his precious mindstones."

Still gripping one of her arms, he shepherded her, not gently, to the door. "And next time you want to see me, Ti-ling, make an appointment."

"But—"

He shut the door in her face and locked it.

Across the room his com board was blinking, lit by a rainbow of calls. The office mech could handle them.

What a morning. He ran his hand through his

sparse bristling hair and thought that maybe he would have that drink early.

* * *

Merrick the Blackbird had settled into his capacious webseat in his lavish apartment and was pondering the morning's fiasco. That assembly with the crowds jeering and Mac pontificating had been a joke. He resolved not to attend any others. It was better to do things behind the scenes.

The door buzzed.

"Come."

Pelleas Karlson's former mistress, Ti-ling, stood in the doorway. Buffed to a high gloss, she shined almost as brightly as the gemstone walls. She was wearing a brilliant orange wrap and some sort of elaborate pants-skirt shot through with silver and purple threads.

"Ah, Ti-ling," he rumbled. "A pleasure, always a pleasure to see a good-looking woman at my door. Come and sit. What's your poison? Or should I just let you choose? You probably know your way around here better than I do."

Instead of looking rattled, she gave him an enigmatic glance, then smiled. "Oh, I'll let you pour. Liageian glowwater. Straight up."

She wore a mindstone ring the size of a small egg. Merrick couldn't keep his gaze off of it. She noticed his attention and smiled. "You like my ring? Pelly gave it to me. One of the last things he gave me." Her eyes glittered with tears. "I treasure it. He told me it was from his own private mine." She held it out for his observation.

Merrick took a good look at it and whistled. "A very sweet rock. And you say that Karlson had his own mines? I didn't know the Styxians ever sold to outsiders."

She shrugged. "He bought them in the last couple of years. The miners were leaving, and I guess they didn't want them anymore. Pelly bought them and sent in mechs."

"These mines. Are they still active?"

Her smile widened. "Funny that you should mention that." She leaned closer and he noticed for the first time that her eyes had emerald flecks within their depths. "You see, Blackbird, the mines are mostly idle at the moment. But they can be started up again. All it takes is a word from the authorities. And the authorities, dear man, are you."

Merrick began laughing. After a moment, Ti-ling joined him. As they subsided, weakly gasping for air, he said, "I think we can manage to work out something. You haven't mentioned these mines to anyone else, have you?"

"Only to Lyle MacKenzie, and he wasn't interested."

Merrick smirked. "No, he wouldn't be." He

paused, considering. MacKenzie might prove to be a problem. But he could be dealt with. And Cristobal might be useful there, after all.

Nodding, Merrick got to his feet and pulled a bottle of fine brandy out of the bar. "Let's toast our new endeavor," he said, handing her a fresh glass.

Ti-ling held up her brandy and said, "To the mines."

Merrick corrected her gently. "To *our* mines."

Chapter Seven

Kayla awoke in the dark. She was lying upon a hard surface, and as she put her hand down she encountered the cool, crumbling rock of the tunnels, unmistakable to the touch.

She had dreamed of Styx, of walking through the cold stone tunnels with her father and mother, prospecting for rich lodes of mindstone. Her mother had rich, dark skin and golden hair that waved above her head like a candlc flame. Her father strode beside her, huge, bearded, burly.

In her high child's voice Kayla had asked: "Why did you stay here? Why, Mama? Why did you stay? Why?"

Her mother had said nothing.

Her father had said, "You don't understand, Katie."

"That's not really my name," she had replied. "Why did you call me that? That's not my name."

Now she lay upon the stone floor for a long while,

sorting through the remembered dream. Her parents? Her sleeping mind had selected Salome and Rab as the templates upon which to hang her parents' roles. And she had been someone younger, smaller, with odd lavender skin.

Memories came swirling up, oddly dreamlike, and yet she knew that these were remembered fragments of real things. The circle of faces. The weeping skeleton. The inquisition by Charon's Eyes. It had happened. Those crazy empaths must have drugged her and left her here.

She sat up slowly, relieved to note that her body was intact and undamaged.

—Golias? Are you here?

—Where else did you think I might be?

—Just checking. Do you have any idea where we are?

—This is your planet, lady. When you get knocked out, I get knocked out as well. If it's possible, I'm more lost now than you are.

Her mouth felt as dry as the tunnel and her stomach grumbled miserably. *—I can't remember the last time I ate.*

—I can. Not recently.

—So they've put us here without food or water.

—I don't think they care much about our survival.

—The bastards! What have I done to them? Nothing.

—It's what they fear that you'll do.

—Whose side are you on?

—With all due respect, I would prefer, if I had a choice, to be on the side of someone with a brighter future.

—Thanks. Shut up, Golias.

She felt a mindtouch, then, weak, wavering, a mere tendril stretching, groping toward her. She opened her mind, reaching for it, but because of the nature of the walls around her, she couldn't be certain of the location of its source.

—Mother?

Again, that tantalizing wisp and its familiar signature, eluding identification.

—Mother, is that you? Can you hear me?

Her mother had been a weak telepath, her empathic power available only on a narrow band. She had been able to communicate with her husband and, occasionally, with Kayla.

—Mother, I'm here! I'm listening. Call me again.

—No.

—Mother, please!

—Not mother.

—If not mother, who?

—Keller. My name is Yates Keller.

For a moment she was dumbstruck. Yates Keller. He was here. That was who she had been talking to, begging him, thinking that he was her mother.

Anger and humiliation blended and became a murderous rage. Kayla jumped to her feet. She would find him and bludgeon him to the stone floor with her bare hands.

In the midst of the red mist fogging her brain, the mindghost, Golias, cut through. *—Wait. He may be useful.*

—Useful? Have you gone crazy?

—Think, Kayla. Alone, we have no chance of getting out of these tunnels alive. With help—even the help of your worst enemy—we might survive and live. Which is more important? Revenge or survival?

—I don't know.

—Then you're not paying attention.

—Golias, it's Yates Keller. He's probably in on this game that Charon's Eyes are playing with us. Waiting with a few of his thugs, hoping to grab me.

—Do you sense any other people down here?

—I told you, my mind powers aren't trustworthy.

—Then perhaps you never really heard Yates Keller either.

—Oh, I know I did. That was unmistakable.

—You can't have it both ways, Kayla.

—I tell you, it was Keller.

—Then let's go find him.

—All right.

She was up and moving through the tunnels, trusting to sound more than nearsense to warn her of the presence of others. Crystals shattered under her feet and cascaded down walls as the noise of her passage fractured fragile rock outcroppings.

—So much for stealth.

—Golias, I'm doing the best I can.

She nearly stumbled over a lump in the middle of the path.

It wasn't rock. It gave when she touched it. A human.

Yates Keller.

Weak, semiconscious, sprawled across the cold stone. She probed him, used mindspeech to awaken him.

—*Who?*

—*Kayla.*

—*Kayla Reed? What are you doing here?*

—*You asked me to come, remember?*

—*Yes. Yes, I think so.*

—*What happened to you?*

He began to lapse into unconsciousness. She shook him, hard.

—*Yates, I said, what happened?*

—*Charon's Eyes. They overwhelmed me, my people. Probably killed them.*

—*Why not you?*

—*Don't know.*

—*Yates, have you seen my mother? My mother, among the other members of Charon's Eyes?*

This seemed to stir him, for his eyes flew open and he stared up at her. —*Your mother? Here?*

Kayla couldn't tell if he was confirming or questioning. Before she could ask again, his eyes closed and his mindspeech slowed to a mumble.

Keller was seriously malnourished, not faking his

weakness as Kayla had at first suspected. It was impossible that he was in league with Charon's Eyes.

She probed him for Salome, Rab, and Arsobades, hoping to learn their location. In his weakened state he should have been an easy read. But Keller's mind was a welter of confusing images and she made little headway.

—Think about them, Yates! Salome, beautiful dark skin, amber eyes. Arsobades, the minstrel.

Yates' eyes stayed closed.

In disgust Kayla released him. He slid down quietly to the tunnel floor and stayed there.

Golias stirred. *—He's in a bad way.*

—He's starving. God only knows how long he's been down here.

—What will you do with him?

It was tempting to leave Keller here, alone, in the dark. But Kayla wanted answers from him and the only way to get them was to keep him alive.

She crouched down and, using her shoulders and thighs for support as Rab had once shown her, grabbed Yates Keller in an over-the-shoulder hold. Slowly she straightened, rising. Pain shot across her shoulders and her back complained from the unexpected load. Keller was lighter than he looked, but his mass still made Kayla stagger.

—Are you crazy? What are you doing?

—What does it look like, Golias? And spare me your observations unless you can help me carry him.

She took a step, teetered, and nearly dropped Keller. She propped him against a wall until she could get the load balanced, took another step, another, and was able to keep moving. She found that as long as she was moving steadily, her awkward burden was much easier to bear.

For how long she moved along blank tunnels she couldn't tell. Her eyes were playing tricks on her in the gloom, and she began to hallucinate strange figures approaching and receding, their outlines barely perceptible.

She knew that if she didn't stop soon she would fall down, but she forced herself to put one foot in front of the other, and, when necessary, leaned against the tunnel walls for support. Keller grew heavier and heavier. Soon she would have to leave him and go on alone.

The wall gave way.

She stumbled, fell, and landed with a thud upon Keller. He groaned for a moment but then subsided.

A faint greenish glow was coming from somewhere above her head. She looked up and saw that it was a glowglobe struggling to come to life.

Another one flickered and blinked. Kayla saw that she had stumbled into an old residence, perhaps some hermit's cave. She didn't know how deep the tunnels ran or who had lived in all of them.

As the lighting improved, she blessed the former inhabitants of the small cave. There were containers of dehydrated foodstuffs, self-heating. The labels had worn away long ago, but the activator tabs were still in place. Kayla triggered one and waited while the food warmed. When it was ready, the lid popped off. She sniffed at the steaming broth that was revealed, took a sip, scalded her tongue, and nearly dropped the container.

—You won't get fed that way.

—Thanks, Golias.

She waited until the broth had cooled, took a sip, another, and finished it in a healthy gulp.

At the scent of the food, Keller groaned and stirred.

Kayla heated another container for him. When it had cooled, she held it under Keller's nose. He groaned again but seemed incapable of feeding himself.

Sighing, she propped him up against her and poured soup into his mouth, waiting for him to swallow.

—If this is how you treat people you hate, I'd like to see how you treat people you really like.

—Shut up, Golias.

Keller took the soup and another packet of it. By the third meal he was able to serve himself.

"Okay," Kayla said. "I want some answers."

Still weak, he nodded.

"What the hell happened to you? What happened to Karlson?"

"It was fine at first. Karlson maintained control. He liked mindstones, but they were just another plaything."

Keller paused, closed his eyes. He swallowed hard and began talking again. "But slowly, he became obsessed by them. Ignored his duties. Mindstones, mindstones, all day long."

Again, he leaned back and closed his eyes.

"Mindstones?" Kayla prompted.

Keller's eyes opened. "Yes. I saw the way things were going, knew it would all end in chaos. Tried to help him reorganize, focus. But he just got deeper and deeper into that stuff."

"How convenient for you."

Keller flinched and looked away. "I didn't hook him on mindsalt. He did it to himself. Became the worst kind of addict. Hollowed out from the inside. I watched it happen."

"And took over."

"Who else? If the public had known, there would have been real civil war. At least I kept things together, kept the machinery running."

"And conveniently hooked him into the groupmind? Suggested that he become the medium, the vector, and destroyed what little was left of his mind. That was kind."

Again Keller would not meet her eyes. "It seemed necessary. The vector of the groupmind died suddenly—and you know how much that group needs a link. You killed one of the earlier vectors."

"Yes," she said. "Poor old Rusty Turlay, my father's friend. And I'm sorry I didn't finish the entire miserable lot of them then. They were miners and you turned them into mindslaves."

"Their day in the mines was over. They weren't doing anybody much good anymore."

"Just like Pelleas Karlson? Well, Yates, at least you're consistent in your reasoning, as repellent as it may be. But explain one thing for me."

"If I can."

"I thought nonempaths couldn't be vectors. How did you turn Karlson into the linkage for the groupmind?"

"Anybody can do it." Keller looked up and Kayla saw a ghost of his old defiant spirit in his eyes. "Anyone who's been exposed to mindstones long enough. It creates enough resonance in their mindfield."

"You wanted to use me that way, once," Kayla said.

"Did I? I can't remnember. But that would have been a stupid waste of your talents."

Kayla let that pass. She had other, more important concerns to deal with, and if she paused to dig up the past, she would finish by burying Yates Keller with it. "Who are these Charon's Eyes people? How did they get here?"

"Some of them stowed away on ore transports.

Others deserted from the mine maintenance staff. A few were already living here in the lower levels and just stayed behind when everybody else emigrated."

"They're crazy."

"And dangerous."

"I think my mother is with them."

"Your mother?" He looked at her as though he thought she had taken leave of her senses.

She ignored his expression and pressed on. "Yes, have you seen her?"

"No."

"Sure?"

"Positive."

The disappointment was crushing. Kayla fought to retain her composure. She had been so sure. . . .

—I told you.

—Just because he hasn't seen her doesn't mean she's not here, Golias.

—But it doesn't mean that she is either.

—And what about your other friends? The ones who disappeared, the crew of the Falstaff? Have you given them up for lost?

—Never!

Kayla focused again on Keller. "Where are Salome, Rab, and Arsobades? And their ship?"

"Safe, all safe. Don't worry."

"Dont' be a fool. Of course I'm worried about them. And I've come here, as you requested."

"Did you bring what I asked?" Greed was a light suddenly flaming in his eyes.

"The Mindstar?" Kayla said coolly. "Of course."

"Where is it?" Keller's voice shook with eagerness.

"In a safe place. Not on me."

"When you give it to me, I'll fulfill my part of the bargain. But first, we have to get out of here."

"And do you know where we are?" Kayla said.

"No." He sounded rueful. "It's deeper than I've been before."

"Me, too."

"We'll do better together than searching separately."

"Yes. Can you walk?"

"I think so." He stood up, wobbling a bit, but managed to remain erect as he took a step. Another. He looked frail, but he was able to move under his own power. Keeping an eye on him, Kayla gathered up some food packs, stuffing them into her suit.

"Okay," she said. "Let's go."

Chapter Eight

The streets of Vardalia were slick with late spring rain. The air was soft and purple in the twilight. Golden beads of lamplight reflected in a puddle.

A pair of boots splashed through and scattered the image. Slowly it re-formed, only to be scattered again, moments later, as a second pair of boots made contact, less emphatically, following the first.

Lyle MacKenzie walked through the purple rain to meet Darius Peters. If he was aware of being followed, he gave little sign, splashing boldly through puddles, walking in the middle of the street.

The Police Minister watched his approach on his office monitor. MacKenzie looked like a man unconcerned for his own safety. Peters sighed and shook his head. The man was a fool.

A moment later, MacKenzie was in his office.

"Mac," Peters said. "How can you be so reckless?"

"Nice to see you, too, Darius. Mind telling me what you're talking about?"

"Safety. Specificially, yours. You should have at least one bodyguard to accompany you at all times. Two would be even better."

"This work has made you paranoid."

"And you're naive, or suicidally stupid." The Police Minister leaned over and pressed a button. "Watch this."

Onscreen, MacKenzie again walked in the street through the rain, and yet he had a shadow. A man, features shielded by a hat, stalked him, steadily following.

"Gods."

Peters nodded. "If he had tried anything I might have been able to stop it, get somebody out there in time. But what happens when you're not within my sphere of influence?"

"You're the Police Minister."

"Now that *is* naive. If I were omnipotent, we wouldn't have a crime to worry about in all of Vardalia. But you know I can't protect you, Mac. Not all the time. Not most of it. So do us all a favor and protect yourself."

"Who do you think was following me?"

"No idea. One of your many enemies." Peters was relieved to see MacKenzie smile knowingly. At least he understood that much.

MacKenzie sighed. "Give me a drink, Darius."

"You like Green Jack?"

"Whatever. Just make it tall."

Peters handed him a chilled container and he opened it, took a long pull, and swallowed. "I can't believe how many enemies an honest man can make by just trying to do his job."

"It's not the job you're doing that bothers them. It's what they're afraid of you doing. Or, rather, undoing."

"You can be plainer than that."

"Look, Mac. There are interests in this city that don't want their deals wrecked. Syndicates. People who want to do business as usual without the interference of newcomers."

MacKenzie held up his free hand. "Then let them. I'm no reformer. I just want the roads to roll."

"But you're not interested in bribes. That unnerves them. They don't trust an honest man."

"For the love of God—"

"It makes sense in a crazy way."

"Only to the truly crazy." MacKenzie finished the beer in two gulps and set it down hard. "All right, you think I'm being foolhardy? Then I'll get a nanny to watch my back." He paused. "You're not seriously suggesting that I take bribes, are you?"

"Of course not."

"Good. The only thing you could bribe me with is an offer to abdicate."

Peters fixed him with a quizzical gaze. "I don't understand. Why did you take this job if you don't want it?"

"I promised somebody."

"That Kate Shadow?"

"Yes."

"I heard she's a bloodthirsty pirate. Ex-con."

"Mostly she's just looking for what's right. And I owe her my life. Several times."

"Sounds like she means a lot to you."

"I'm not in love with her, if that's what you're getting at. But she asked me to do something. And by God, I said I would, so I will."

Peters nodded. "A word of friendly advice, then. Annnounce elections soon. Let the people see that you're not power hungry. Invite the union reps to your office. Let them see that you want to hear about their concerns. You're a stranger now, Mac. Make yourself familiar."

"You make it sound as if you think I'll have this job for a while."

"You might—if you're lucky. But I didn't ask you to meet me to discuss your professional future. I want to talk about the mindsalt trade."

"Mindsalt?" MacKenzie reared back in his seat. "What about it?"

"It's destroyed Vardalia, and the Alliance. I want to get it out of here. Now that the mines are dead, there's finally a chance to end it. Supplies will run out. I want to hit the places that store it and sell it."

MacKenzie stared at him with surprise and renewed respect. "I didn't think you were such a reformer, Darius. Thought you turned a blind eye to the salt trade in the past."

"Had to. There was no hope of limiting it while Pelleas Karlson was alive. But I love this city, Mac. I want it to survive. And now Karlson is dead."

"Well, you may love Vardalia, but I certainly don't."

"Maybe not, but you've seen the horrors of mindsalt addiction, haven't you? Seen what it does to people."

"You just said that the mines are closed. The supply will run out. That should take care of it."

"Maybe. But the word on the street is that certain interests want to reopen the mines."

"Those syndicates you were mentioning?"

"Maybe. Certainly it'll take one to get production and distribution up and going."

"And what do you want from me?"

"Your cooperation. And your help."

Lyle MacKenzie looked across the desk at the Police Minister. The man cared. He was dedicated. And MacKenzie needed his help if he was going to keep one step ahead of Merrick the Blackbird. "Okay. I'm in it with you." MacKenzie held out his hand. Peters grasped it firmly. "And the gods help us both."

* * *

Piles of mindstones. They sprawled across the tables, onto the seat cushions and floor, winking, glowing, promising untold pleasures. The room was filled with a red-blue-bronze radiance from the secret hoard that had belonged to Pelleas Karlson.

Merrick had seen many a mindstone before, but even he was impressed by the sheer quantity and quality arrayed before him. He grabbed one at random, a gem the size of his fist, held it up to the light, and admired it, nodding. "Very nice. Very fine, indeed. I'll say one thing for Karlson, he knew his gems."

"And there's more waiting to be mined," said Ti-ling. "Waiting for you—and me."

Merrick smiled. "Once we have our partnership established, we'll empty out that planet faster than you can say mining mech."

"I don't see why you don't trust me, Merrick. Why do we need all these legal agreements?"

"Nothing personal, my dear. I don't trust anybody. Never have. Never will."

Ti-ling frowned as though she were planning to pout, but then her face cleared and she managed a smile. "You're a cynic, Merrick. Worse than Pelly."

"I never claimed to be anything but."

"You sound proud."

"I'm not ashamed, if that's what you mean."

He watched Ti-ling gather herself for what he assumed would be another seductive assault. She was accustomed to winning and to manipulating powerful men. But Merrick had no intention of becoming

Pelleas Karlson's replacement—at least so far as Ti-ling was concerned. Besides, he didn't like ambitious women, no matter how beautiful. They were too dangerous.

She leaned toward him, lips parted.

Gently he straight-armed her, forcing her back into her seat.

"What the hell's wrong with you, Merrick?" Murderous fires danced with green flames in her dark eyes.

"Again, my dear, nothing personal. But I like to keep business relationships separate from others of a more intimate nature."

She opened her mouth to say something, but the door buzzer cut her off.

"I'm Mr. Popularity today." Merrick checked the doorscreen and saw the agents Raintree and Fichu waiting.

"What is it?" he rasped.

"We have the results of the union negotiations to discuss," Raintree said. "Among other things."

"Come back later. Or take them to Mac."

"We need a decision right away."

"Later."

Fichu saw Ti-ling behind Merrick and his mouth opened in shock. He nudged his companion.

Raintree frowned. In a whisper, she said, "Don't trust her! Don't make any deals with her—"

"I'll make deals with anybody I like." Merrick shut down the screen.

The buzzer went off again. He ignored it. Irritated now, he swung around to Ti-ling. "And don't you push me on those mines, hear? We'll get the paperwork finished, and they'll open when they open, not a moment sooner."

Chapter Nine

It galled Kayla fiercely to be walking through the tunnels of her home world beside the very man she had sworn to kill. Worse yet was to be forced into an alliance with him against their mutual enemies, the fanatic members of Charon's Eyes.

She didn't trust Keller, didn't want him at her side much less guarding her back.

He had caused her family nothing but woe. He was a murderer and liar, a blackmailer who had kidnapped her friends, destroyed his benefactor, and enslaved people he had once called neighbors.

He was also her only hope if the members of Charon's Eyes returned to attack them.

"You still think it looks unfamiliar?" Keller said.

"I told you," she said sharply. "I've never been in this area before. And it's been years since I tunnel-walked."

Keller gave a brief nod. "I knew that Karlson's mechs had cut a new network of tunnels, but I never expected them to be so deep, or so complex."

The tunnel turned left and they walked past a row of deactivated mechs, through a deep-cut doorway, and into a vast cavern filled with looming crystalline protrusions and chandeliers.

A feeble glowglobe cast a greenish light and threw long shadows along the steeply-raked floor.

Kayla was suddenly reminded of another crystalline cavern on a distant asteroid, where a prison guard named Mogul had fallen to his death.

She remembered, too, her more recent interrogation by the members of Charon's Eyes. They had called her Sister Blood. The name stuck in her mind.

Were they right? Was she bloodthirsty? A killer?

No, no, she had tried to save Mogul. Not that he had deserved it. When she had killed before, she had had no choice. She didn't enjoy it.

Kayla forced her attention outward, to the hard rock surrounding her and Keller.

Signs of excavation were everywhere: rounded boreholes, shallow terraced pits, and a silky-smooth segment of rock that looked as though it had melted and frozen into gentle ripples.

A ramp of flexible mesh took them over a declivity, a chasm whose jagged lips would have made for splintered and uncertain footing.

They walked on, out of the cavern, through dark spirals of rock and jagged passageways that seemed newly cut. Kayla felt as if she were walking upon a stone treadmill, making no progress.

"What a hellhole this planet is," Keller said.

Kayla was tempted to agree with him. Aside from a certain sentimental tie, she felt no love for Styx. And yet some of her happiest memories had been formed there. And some of her worst.

"Do you have any idea where we are, Kayla?"

"Will you kindly stop asking me? My suit compass is going crazy because of the odd magnetic fields down here. I can't get any kind of fix. When I see something I recognize, I'll tell you."

They came around a corner that looked familiar. Heartened, Kayla moved a bit faster, pulling ahead of Keller.

The ground fell away.

She was up to her neck in mounds of soft flaking stuff that held her helpless, immobilized.

"Yates," she cried. "It's a dust pit."

She heard him swear.

Dust pits were treacherous by-products of the mining process and the natural erosion of the tunnels. The pulverized rock, ground into exceedingly fine particles, collected in pools that appeared solid until you had stepped into them.

Keller's father had perished, suffocated, in one. His mother would have suffered the same fate if not for the intervention of Redmond Reed, Kayla's father.

Keller stood, unmoving, obviously terrified.

"Dammit, Yates, come on. Pull me out!"

"I can't."

Kayla floundered, slipping. There was no purchase for her feet, none at all. She would disappear beneath the surface, drown in the dust. "Yates!"

He made a choking sound but didn't move.

Fear couldn't be reasoned with, and Kayla didn't try. Desperately she summoned a coercive surge of mindpower and grabbed him up in it, moving his arms, his legs, his entire body as though he were a huge puppet.

—*Your jacket. Take it off.*

The jacket came off.

—*Tie a knot in one end. Hurry!*

He knotted one end of it into a good-sized lump.

—*Hold one end, toss the knotted one to me.*

As the knot swung over Kayla's head, she reached up a leaden arm and snagged it.

—*Pull, dammit. Pull!*

Holding fast to the jacket, Kayla had Yates back away from the lip of the pit. As she urged him on, he dragged her, inch by inch, out of the dust, over the jagged rocks, and onto safe footing.

She gazed up at his face and saw that it was still frozen with fear. Disgusted, she released her mindhold on him. "Thanks for nothing."

Keller shook himself like a wet bambera. His composure was instantly back in place. "Sorry. Your mindhold was very effective. But you always were a stronger empath than I was."

"And don't forget it," Kayla snapped.

"Why should I? It's been useful before, and I think it'll be useful again. It's why I suggested that we team up."

She didn't like the way he said that but decided to let it go. If she challenged him on everything he said to her, she would eventually push him into a dust pit.

They wandered for what felt like hours. Now and again she would pass a stump, a crystalline outcropping, or a bend in the road that seemed familiar. But there were not enough clues to enable her to put together a route for them out of the tunnels.

Finally she saw a number of familiar-looking markings in the walls and said, "I think I've got it now."

Left at the junction. Right by that blackened stalagmite stump. Left at the broken arch.

Right into a dead end.

"Damn. I was sure that this was the way."

Keller said nothing, merely sighed, but that was indictment enough.

"You think you can do better?" Kayla snapped.

"Did I say anything?"

"You didn't have to."

"It's not polite to read thoughts without permission."

"Dammit, Yates, for two credits, I'd leave you here to rot in the dark."

"But you won't."

"Don't push your luck."

She would have said more, but her attention was drawn to a stump up ahead. Dark crystal, gleaming with green inclusions. It looked like Old Bart's Nose.

Kayla's spirits leaped even as she told herself that she was probably mistaken, this path would just lead to a dead end, too.

But the next turn, and the turn after that, led exactly where she had expected.

Left. Right. Right again.

The tunnel sloped uphill now. Glowglobes set into the walls were actually functioning. And the distinct and steady hum of machinery set up a corresponding echo in the crystalline walls around them.

"Come on." Kayla moved faster now. They would find their way out—she recognized this area, she knew where they were. It was a section distant from her family's home and holdings, but familiar nonetheless. "Move it, Yates."

The mindghost, Golias, began to whisper to her. —*What will you do about him?*

Before she replied, she made certain that she was properly shielded. Keller was a weak empath, but that didn't mean he couldn't catch her thoughts on a narrow probe.

—I don't know. I haven't found out what I wanted. Where Salome and the others are. Once I do, he's finished.

—He saved your life back there.

—Bullshit, Golias. I saved my life, using him.

—You may need him again before this is over.

—I hope you're wrong.

—Don't be reckless.

—Never, unless I have no other choice.

"You know where you're going," Keller said.

"If I've got it figured right, we'll come out by the edge of the old Guild Hall."

"We'll be targets out in the open."

"You sound like you're awfully afraid of these lunatics."

"Just because they're crazy doesn't mean they're not dangerous."

What else he might have said was lost in the sudden whisper of cloth moving through air, feet moving through tunnels.

Charon's Eyes, the fanatics, searching for them?

Kayla grabbed Yates by the arm and yanked him off the path and back behind a towering crystal stalagmite.

A flurry of footsteps grew louder, nearer.

Kayla made mind contact with Keller.

—I count five of them. Do you feel strong enough for a fight?

He nodded.

—On my signal.

She waited until the last of the fanatics had passed, then crept out behind them, nodding for Keller to follow.

Kayla launched a quick, numbing mindattack and the fanatic closest to her, a slender woman with braided white hair, went limp. Kayla grabbed her and passed her to Keller, who set her out of sight.

The next, a tall, thin man, all bones and angles, was easily subdued.

As Kayla began to work on the third, a new sound erupted in the tunnels and a group of cowl-wearing empaths appeared. The leader was Natan. His pale eyes locked with Kayla's.

"Grab them!"

Kayla dropped the empath nearest to her and kicked the next one in the throat. Crystal cracked and broke with sharp musical notes. Shards of pulverized mindsalt snowed down in a glittering storm. Keller was struggling with a burly, bearded albino. She knew that Natan would try to form a groupmind to subdue them, so she had perhaps seconds left to act.

Without waiting to ask permission, she grabbed hold of Keller's mind and used it to augment her own mindpower, channeling everything the two of them had into forming a complete and absorbing illusion.

A huge demon towered over them, a ritual warrior with bloody runes engraved into his cheeks and forehead. His lipless mouth opened to reveal pointed teeth as sharp as swords. His eyes blazed with terrible fires. And where his chest and guts should have been was instead a cage filled with gaunt and hollow-eyed prisoners. Their faces were those of the members of Charon's Eyes.

Kayla had the thing exhale mind-numbing energy, scrambling the brains of the other empaths. The creature set tiny fire imps dancing in their eyes, plucking at their deepest fears, sending them into mounting panic.

Out of the shadows came lumbering jailers without faces, reaching with spidery hands to scoop them up and imprison them in the demon warrior's chest.

When she cleared the image, not a member of Charon's Eyes remained in the tunnel.

Keller's face was drained of color. "Ye gods, you don't fool around, do you?" he whispered.

Kayla smiled a feral smile.

"Where did they go?"

"If they're smart, they made for the deepest tunnels. And they'll stay there, unless they want another taste."

She leaned back, panting. Why did she feel so warm? The air all around her had turned pink and aromatic, as though she were inside a giant flower. Her heart beat with an urgent rhythm.

Then it came to her. Mindsalt. In the air. All around them. They had breathed it in. Swallowed it.

Beside her, Keller was breathing hard as well.

And the years melted away: she remembered the first time she had really looked at Yates Keller, seen the handsome features made somehow more appealing by the arrogant manner. The dark eyes. The full lips. Had longed for him without really knowing then what it was that she had longed for.

Had dreamed, once, of how it would be if they were together, coupled.

And he had touched her then, kissed her. She knew the taste of his lips, the strength of his arms, the spice of his skin.

He was her enemy. She had sworn to kill him. And at the moment she could think of nothing better to do than wrap her arms around him and tear off his clothing.

She fought off the impulse.

Turned and caught his eye.

He was thinking the same thing. She knew it.

Then there was no time left to think.

They were in each other's arms, rolling across the tunnel floor to fetch up against the base of Old Bart's Nose. They were kissing deep and long, melding their flesh until it wasn't clear where one left off and the other began.

Their clothing came off quickly. The chill air of the tunnels was merely stimulating as they wrestled and clung, gasping. It was a wild, primal act in which they clawed their way together to climax after climax.

A tiny voice in Kayla's brain was shouting at her, asking her what she thought she was doing, but it was very faint and soon it went away.

Chapter Ten

It was a busy night at the Pink Eye. The regulars packed the bar, drinking and laughing. The mindriders had a line waiting that half-circled the room. Credits piled up in the cash box as the mechband wailed:

> "Don't make me unhappy,
> Gimme some salt,
> I wanna be happy, baby,
> Open your vault,
> I know where it's hidden
> I know what to do,
> Gimme some salt, baby,
> I got the blues."

The private room for mindsalt and breen sales, open for a special fee, was standing room only. The power shift in Vardalia had left everybody feeling a little nervous.

Coral Raintree and Robard Fichu were in the small room, feeling considerably less nervous than they had upon arrival. Mindsalt helped with that.

When the first police officer entered, Coral Raintree nodded in recognition—a former colleague, probably just doing some nosing around or looking for a pick-him-up.

When the arrests began, she watched in shock, her mind refusing to coordinate her limbs, to move her body in self-protective flight. Fichu plucked at her sleeve.

"Coral, it's time to go." He shook her gently. "Coral!"

A glass smashed and a woman began screaming.

Raintree remembered the use of her legs. Out the back door into the rainy night. Between buildings she saw the clustered police vehicles, already filling with Pink Eye patrons.

"Where to?" Fichu asked.

"Merrick. The Blackbird'll want to know."

* * *

Merrick paced the rooms of his luxurious apartment, a man enraged. Damage reports came in every few minutes and each was worse than the last.

Ti-ling sat upon a sofa, coolly finishing a smoke stick and elaborately ignoring Coral Raintree and Robard Fichu.

"Not only the barkeeper," Raintree said. "But the owner and even the bouncer are in custody. At least half the customers. Anybody with an ounce of mindsalt on them. And two other bars that you have an interest in were hit: Woman in the Wall and The Sleeping Gypsy."

Fichu nodded. "The word's out. Somebody's targeted the mindsalt trade."

"But that's always been immune," said Merrick. "Strictly hands-off."

"That was before."

"Why now?" Merrick bellowed. "What's the point of destroying these tiny bits of business?"

Raintree shrugged. "It happens. Some official complains. Then there are raids. Bars close. It cools off. Bars open again."

"Why didn't I know about this beforehand?"

"The police aren't under *your* jurisdiction," said Tiling. "Are they?"

Merrick stared at her, hard. "You're right. It's Mac. Mac's got to be doing it."

Ti-ling warmed to the topic. "He probably heard that we were going to reopen the mines and wants to scare us. As if it's any of his business what we do."

"You think that's what's behind it?" Merrick's dark eyes glowed with fury.

"What else? He knows you're the real power in Vardalia now. He's probably scared and trying to intimidate you."

Merrick smirked. "He'll have to work harder if that's what he's up to."

"Those operators will be furious—they were promised immunity," Fichu said. "Somebody told me that Darius Peters is threatening to close them down and keep them closed."

Ti-ling smiled. "I'll handle Darius."

Merrick gave her a quick approving glance. "Good."

"There's one other complication," Raintree said.

"What's that?"

"More like who. Cristobal."

"What about him?"

"He was one of the first arrested. Amped on mindsalt from the look of him."

"Damn fool." Merrick nodded. It confirmed his suspicions. Trust Cristobal to have developed a mindsalt habit. "Well, that clinches it. Mac has got to be behind this, persecuting Cris." He sighed, reached into his pocket and extracted a credit chip. "Here, Fichu. Spring him, will you? And bring him back here."

Raintree and Fichu stood, ready to leave. Merrick held up his hand, stopping them. "You two can give Ti-ling a lift home, can't you?"

Ti-ling's eyes flared with anger, but she looked down quickly, smothering the blaze. Gathering herself, she flounced out in a cloud of perfume. "I'll talk to you tomorrow, Merrick."

"Fine. Let me know where you get with Peters."

He dismissed all three of them without a backward glance.

* * *

The former coleader of the War Minstrels walked jauntily—a bit too jauntily—into Merrick's rooms. He beamed approval, brown eyes shining.

"Very nice," Cristobal said. "You always did have good taste, Merrick. And now I see that it was even better than I thought. Or should I include Karlson in the compliment? These walls, I didn't notice them before. What are they composed of? Looks like opaline crystal. The cabochon form is interesting in these patterns, but I would have selected black ivorine to frame the inlay rather than blue ceramsteel."

Merrick rolled his eyes at Raintree and Fichu. "You said he was amped. Not cruising at jump speed."

"It'll wear off in a few hours," said Raintree.

"Not soon enough. I suppose I'm his keeper until then."

The two agents made as if to sit down, but Merrick waved them away. "Go home, or wherever it is you go at this hour. I'll talk with you tomorrow."

He shut the door heavily.

Cristobal, babbling to himself, was running his hands along the walls, nodding, smiling, spouting a steady critique. "Such workmanship. You don't see this now. Couldn't afford to have it done. That's the appeal of old things, isn't it? Recalls a simpler, better world."

"Cris," Merrick said. "Come sit down, old friend. Take the weight off your feet."

Cristobal didn't even hear him.

"Cris!" He reached out and snagged his arm. "Come. Sit. Down." He forced him into a webseat.

Cristobal made to get up and follow him.

"Stay! I'll be right back."

He entered his study, grabbed the autodoc box, and hurried back into the main room.

Cristobal had activated all the wallscreens and was singing along with three of them.

Merrick hit the master switch and locked the screens off. Then he set the autodoc to mixing a tranquilizer.

Cristobal, humming madly, was dancing, doing a series of quick steps, kicks, and twirls.

Merrick reconsidered. He wanted Cristobal alert, not manic. Quickly he punched a different command on the box, canceling the first and reordering. In a moment the autodoc's ready light flashed blue. "Hold out your arm."

Cristobal did as he was told.

Merrick pressed a hypo bulb against it.

"What was that?"

"Something to calm you down."

"I'm calm. Who says that I'm not calm? I'm perfectly calm, Merrick."

"In a degla's eye."

"You're the one who's tense, Merrick. You really should relax more."

"Like you? No thanks." Merrick lit up another smoke stick and sat beside Cristobal, staring into his eyes. "Now try to pay attention. We're going to have a little chat, Cris. Which means that I'll talk and you'll listen."

"All right."

"We've got a problem."

"We do?"

"I said, *I'll* talk."

Cristobal nodded meekly.

"Our problem has a name, Cris, one well known to you. Lyle MacKenzie. He's the reason the mindsalt trade is drying up and the reason why you ended up in the hoosegow tonight."

A slight frown creased Cristobal's face. "Mac, a problem? What are you talking about?"

"I mean, old buddy, that Mac is gunning for you. It's obvious. He'll hound you, day or night. You think that raid on the Pink Eye was an accident?"

"I heard that the Police Minister was leaning on the mindsalt sellers."

"That's what Mac wants you to think. It's a cover, man. Don't you see it?"

Suspicion began to glimmer in Cristobal's eyes and

he suddenly seemed just a trifle more focused. "Mac planned it? Planned the raid to get me?"

"Precisely."

As Cristobal's drug haze began to dissipate, Merrick bore down on him. "And if I hadn't bailed you out in time, you'd probably be sitting in the deepest, darkest pit of a dungeon that can be found in Vardalia."

"I'm grateful. You know that."

"But you're not safe, boy. Not yet. Tonight is just the beginning. He'll be after you now, won't let up, not for a minute. It can only end one way."

Suddenly Cristobal sat up, mouth set, eyes clear, and fixed his gaze firmly on Merrick.

"One way," he said.

Merrick leaned closer, cocking his head at a conspiratorial angle. "It's become a matter of self-preservation, Cris. Protection. I think you understand what I'm saying."

"It's him or me."

The Blackbird nodded. "And let's be practical. With Mac eliminated, there'll be fewer folk to divide the pie."

Cristobal's jaw jutted. "I know what to do."

"You sure now?"

"Leave Mac to me."

Merrick patted him on the shoulder. "Attaboy."

Chapter Eleven

It was like awakening from a bad dream. Kayla found herself lying naked in Yates Keller's arms. Her head was throbbing, but the rest of her body had turned to ice. She was freezing. Unceremoniously she pulled free from Keller's grasp and yanked on her pressure suit, turning up the thermostat.

Keller awoke and made haste to dress as well. Although he averted his gaze from hers, there was a smug look on his face that infuriated Kayla.

Bastard, she thought. *Taking advantage of me like that.*

—You were quite eager, as I recall.

—Golias, you miserable voyeur. Don't you ever get tired of watching other people's intimacies?

—Certainly, but what choice do I have? I understand your remorse and disgust, Kayla. But let me assure you that in the heat of the moment you seemed to be enjoying yourself.

—Yeah, well, stuff that memory down your disembodied throat and gag on it.

After that the mindghost wisely remained quiet.

Keller was the first to break the awkward silence in the chamber.

"I'd like to show you something."

She nodded, managing not to meet his eyes.

He led her to a warren of recently-cut rooms, pressed his palm to a lock, and as the door slid open, preceded her into the chamber. "Here. Turn right."

She moved from light into darkness, and into light again as the inset wallglobes lit, reacting to human presence.

Kayla took one look and gasped.

The room glittered with unearthly radiance, red-blue and bronze. Mindstones lay scattered across tables, piled into holding pens like so many glass marbles. Cutting mechs and other delicate machinery lined the walls.

There was an incredible fortune strewn about the room. "What is this?" Kayla demanded.

"Karlson's private lab."

"On Styx? Since when?"

"He had it put in when the mines were automated. This is why I wanted you to come here to meet me."

Kayla stared in amazement at the chatoyancy meters and refraction generators. Laser cutters. Diamond mirrors. "Karlson had some nice toys."

"More than toys," Keller said, frowning. "He was serious, deadly serious, about mindstones. And to give him credit, he alone accomplished what generations of thick-skulled Styxians couldn't—or wouldn't—do."

"Which was?"

"Solved the secret of mindstones: learned how to manipulate them, use them, cut them. He saw the importance of asterism—you know, that special glow in the heart of the best stones. Karlson realized that it was an amplifier for the stones' power. That's why the Mindstar was so strong. But Karlson died before he could put that knowledge to use."

"Or he was helped along the way."

Keller's expression was that of an innocent newborn. "Don't blame me for Karlson's death, Kayla. I didn't do it. He became a mindsalt addict. If anything, I tried to stop him."

"I'll just bet you did."

"He was useful, dammit! And I wasn't ready to take over. Not then."

"I suppose that's the most remorse that you're capable of, Yates."

"Stop baiting me, Kayla." The frustration in his voice sounded genuine. "Don't you see that we can do this together? Don't you see what an opportunity this is for us?"

"Do what, you idiot? Control the Three Systems? Hook everybody on mindsalt?"

"Don't be ridiculous. But Karlson's theories about the ways to cut mindstones and utilize them—we can use that. Build an empire together. The Three Systems Alliance is finished, Kayla. It's all falling apart. The moment's come for a strong leader. Your mind-powers coupled with my knowledge of the mind-stones could provide the strength and vision that's needed now. You have the loyalty of the rebels. I can deal with the Old Guard." He reached out to her, imploring.

Kayla deftly avoided his outstretched arms. "You want to use me, Yates. Just as you always did. That's my appeal for you. You only think you want to be with me. But you're fooling yourself. And you nearly fooled me, once."

"Oh, really?" His eyes cut holes in her. "And what was that all about back there? Nobody forced you to lie down with me. You wanted it, Kayla. Wanted it as much as I did."

"That was the mindsalt."

"Kayla, don't you see?" There was a desperate note to his persuasive tone now, growing louder. "We were meant to be together. Don't fight it."

"Be together?" Her voice cracked over the words. "And live here, underground, in Styx, surrounded by all of our happy, happy memories?"

"Don't be foolish. We can live anywhere. Do anything. *Listen* to me, Kayla. Karlson discovered how to create temporary empaths. He analyzed and reconfigured faceting patterns. He experimented with cabochon mindstones and learned that they could counteract other mindstones' effects, even nullify the powers of some empaths. Doesn't that tell you anything?"

"Yes. That he was even more dangerous than I ever dreamed. That he should have been stopped long ago."

Keller didn't seem to hear her. He was lost in his dreams of a new galactic order. "Now that you've brought the Mindstar, we can use what Karlson learned, create what he foresaw. In a way, it's his legacy."

She stared at him with a mixture of pity and dismay. "You really believe that, don't you?"

"The Mindstar." He snapped his fingers eagerly. "Do you have it?"

"Yes," she said truthfully. "But not on me."

"On your shuttle?"

"My shuttle crashed."

He grabbed her. "Don't play games with me, Kayla. Where is that stone?"

"In orbit. Safe." Calmly, she pulled his hand away from her shoulder. "And where are my friends, Yates? Where are Salome and the rest?"

Keller shrugged. "What difference does it make? They're not important, now."

And so she knew. He had killed them, killed the people who had taken her in when she was alone and an outlaw, on the run. Sheltered her after her own parents had perished at Keller's hands. He was death twice over. And she had slept with him, this murderer of her friends and family.

Kayla didn't stop to think, to reason, to argue with herself. Gathering her mindpowers, she struck.

The room shook as she enveloped Keller in a mind-storm of astonishing proportions. Never before had she summoned such a storm, fed such a power wave. Perhaps the mindstones all around served to refract and reflect the power of Kayla's mind.

The storm sizzled around Keller, reflecting like green lightning from the walls of the chamber.

"No!" Keller cried. "Kayla, stop!"

She struck at him again.

Keller screamed. Beyond speech now, he held out his arms, tried feebly to ward off the blows that were hammering him.

Kayla slashed and pounded. Keller was an insect, a microbe, a monster. He would be swallowed alive, burned, flayed, every bone in his body broken a thousand times for his treacheries. She invaded his mind, pulled out his deepest fears, and fed them to him, one by one.

The slow death by fire.

The maiming torture.

The suffocation in the dark.

How do you like that, Yates? And how about this one?

He screamed again and fell to his kness.

Die, she thought. *Miserable bastard, die!*

Somewhere deep in her own mind, Golias was yelling, trying desperately to get her attention.

She lashed out once more.

With a mortal gasp, Keller fell to the hard stone floor. He lay, face up, eyes open but unseeing.

And Kayla stared, frozen and suddenly frightened.

What had she done? What had she done?

"Yates?"

There was no answer.

She felt a wild urge to laugh, but she knew that if she utterd a sound, any sound at all, it would turn into a shredding, unending shriek.

Again. She had done it again. Exactly like her first attack on Keller, in these very tunnels, so long ago. Had she learned nothing, nothing at all, in all the years since?

Sister Blood. Did the name truly fit?

Chapter Twelve

The word had gone out along the space lanes that Vardalia was no longer the wide-open, welcoming city it had been under Pelleas Karlson's rule.

Honest traders were admitted to Vardalia Port as usual, berthed their ships, and made prosperous tours of the city, dealing their goods.

Prostitutes and pimps, dealers in flesh, were also free to ply their trade, as were the cyberpalace mounts, the laser stimmers, trode masseurs, proxy mates, and all the other merchants of good-times-by-the-hour.

But sellers of mindstones and mindsalt were put on notice: such trade was now forbidden and establishments that allowed it would be shut down. The fastest guarantee of a one-way trip to jail was to offer mindsalt on the street. No one could be trusted: informers were paid an unofficial "courtesy fee." Wives turned in husbands, children reported their parents.

And so nightlife in Vardalia continued. But it was less raucous, neater, and its purveyors kept several watchful eyes open for police.

* * *

As the double suns sank behind Vardalia's white towers, Police Minister Darius Peters and Lyle MacKenzie huddled together in Peters' office.

"It's a start," said the minister. "We're letting people know how things are."

"Never thought I'd see myself as a reformer," MacKenzie said wryly. "You're that worst of all possible things, Darius: a good influence on me."

Peters' lips quirked, but his dark eyes remained serious. "We can expect repercussions, Mac."

"There goes your paranoia again."

"One man's paranoia is just another man's hard reading of the facts."

"Hah!"

"Don't pretend to be naive, Mac. You don't have any right to that act."

"Maybe so. But I'll be damned if I'll see a shadow behind every window, in every doorway."

"You're not a cop."

"No, I'm just a simple rebel and ex-con, thank the gods for small favors."

Peters refused to be deflected. "You *should* keep

watch for shadows behind you, Mac. I've told you that before."

MacKenzie's rejoinder was drowned out by the bustle and clatter at the door of Peters' office. A loud officious voice belonging to Ramon, Peters' private secretary, could be heard, saying, "Nobody's to go in there."

A woman's voice rose in protest, the words unclear but the tone most apparent.

Seconds later, a buzzer went off on the minister's private com board.

"Yes?" Peters rasped.

"A Miss Ti-ling is here, sir, and quite insistent on seeing you. Extremely insistent."

"Doesn't that woman believe in making appointments?" MacKenzie said, his voice rising. "I'm glad to see it's you she's after, for a change."

Peters frowned at him, but there was an odd glint in his eyes as he addressed the com board: "Tell her she'll have to wait, Ramon. Make it stick."

"She says that it's urgent."

"She'll wait like everyone else without an appointment, until I have a free moment. Or come back another day."

Again, beyond the wall, a woman's voice could be heard, strident, demanding. But the com board remained silent. And finally the woman's voice died away.

"That's better," Peters said. "Back to business." He

settled deeper into his chair. "Seventeen clubs have been raided, Mac. We closed eight of them and shut down the salt trade in the rest. Bribes aren't working, and a stay in jail can be expensive for a club owner."

"That leaves how many to go?"

"You mean the ones that are still known to sell mindsalt? Six. Only six."

MacKenzie nodded with satisfaction. "Another week and we should see the end of the mindsalt trade in central Vardalia."

"Then we'll work on the outskirts," Peter said.

"Ambitious, aren't you?" MacKenzie shook his head. "Received any death threats yet?"

"Two or three."

"Not very impressive."

"Give them time."

"What about bribes?"

Peters laughed. "I could have retired and bought myself a neat little orbital estate."

"Sounds tempting."

"Only until you've seen one."

"Peters, you sound almost jovial." A buzzer went off as Mac's belt. "Got to go. Dinner meeting with the ramp-fitters union officials. I'll leave you to Tiling. Just show me the back way out of here."

Peters waved him across the room where a door led MacKenzie into another office, and an exit that bypassed Peters' reception area. Two guards stood beside the door and saluted as he went past. Feeling faintly ridiculous, MacKenzie saluted back.

* * *

"Darius, why did you make me wait?" Ti-ling was all pout as she entered the room.

Peters watched her approach and marveled at her beauty. But then, he had always found Ti-ling beautiful, had envied Pelleas Karlson his mistress, and never imagined that one day Karlson might be gone.

Ti-ling wore nearly transparent layers of golden robes that shimmered as she walked. Her skin seemed a golden extension of her garments. Would it feel as silken? Peters wondered.

In the past he and Ti-ling had maintained a playful flirtation, and as he saw her dark eyes sparkling now, he was hard put to feel any irritation over her disregard for his schedule. Why should she care? She was worth special consideration.

"Forgive me. It *was* inconsiderate," he said. "I suppose that I should cancel all my appointments to keep my time free just in case you drop by."

"Now you're teasing me." She drew nearer, so close that he could smell the delicate spice of her perfume. Or, he wondered, did her skin just naturally smell that good?

"I'd be happy to keep time free for you every day,

you know." His tone was light, but his eyes strove to lock onto hers.

Her gaze eluded him. "And would I have to check in at your front desk and talk to your nasty assistant?"

"Only if you were coming in on official business. Is this official?"

Now her glance did meet his and held, emerald glimmering in deepest onyx. "No," she said. Her voice had gone low and husky. "I wanted to ask you a question."

"Ask."

"Why have you been avoiding me?"

"Avoiding you?" He sat back, thunderstruck.

"Now that Pelly's gone."

Peters groped for words. "Ti-ling, the last thing I want to do is avoid you. But I assumed that you were . . . busy."

"Well, your assumption was wrong." She came around to his side of the desk and leaned against the desktop, staring at him. The message in her eyes was unmistakable. "Ever since Pelly died, I've been waiting for you to call. Finally, I got tired of waiting." She reached out, put her arms around his neck, and pressed her soft lips against his.

Peters crushed her against him as the room began to spin.

* * *

Almost immediately Lyle MacKenzie realized that he was being followed. The footsteps behind him echoed loudly, shifting in rhythm as his did, reacting to every change of tempo he made.

The street, a lively marketplace at noon, was deserted now. Purple shadows filled it, and every window had its shutters drawn. No hope of help here.

He quickened his pace, finding strength in fear, and sped down the street, scanning for escape routes. An alley. He made for it quickly.

His pursuer was right behind him, but he dared not waste the time to turn his head and see who it was.

He was running flat out, around a corner, through a narrow passage, behind gutted news kiosks.

Now he heard two sets of footsteps pounding behind him, not taking care to mask direction or intent.

MacKenzie reached for his disruptor only to grasp empty air at his waist. He had left it in his desk. *Fool,* he thought. *Mrs. MacKenzie has a fool for a son.*

The street tapered up ahead and he feared he had reached a dead end.

Could he double back toward the Police Ministry? Unlikely. Not with two men on his trail.

The rasp of a disruptor sounded behind him.

He ducked and saw a wall where he had stood blasted into tiny pieces.

On hands and knees MacKenzie scrabbled away. The pavement scraped his palms raw.

Move, move, move!

He rolled through a pile of stinking garbage and under the rusted carapace of a junked skimmer.

Temporary shelter.

Don't relax, man. Just breathe.

Clinging to the rusted skimmer skeleton like armor and shield, MacKenzie made the shelter of a trader's shuttered booth.

If he called out, would anyone hear? And if they did, would they help him or just lock themselves away deeper behind their closed shutters?

The skimmer skeleton rattled in his hands, dragging against the road beneath his feet.

Idiot, he thought. *A disruptor bolt can go through this skimmer frame like a knife through a butter pot.* But he felt safer under it, just the same.

The footsteps behind him grew louder.

It sounded as though there were more of them, coming closer, trying to surround him.

Again a disruptor hissed and spat.

Missed.

Stupid, he thought, *to cower here, waiting for the end.*

Another shot, another miss.

Dammit!

MacKenzie stood, roaring his defiance, and tossed his carapace at shadowy figures, heard it connect, and somebody cry out. But he was moving, out of range, around the nearest corner, running for his life.

Zap!

A bolt took out a chunk of masonry just behind him.

Guns popped across the street, echoes confusing him: how many were firing?

Metal splinters. Fragments of ceramsteel. MacKenzie was peppered with them, could feel them itching and prickling at his scalp, on his skin. Felt, too, the trickle and slickness of blood: just a few cuts, nothing major. He had been lucky, so far.

Gods, let that luck hold.

He was in the Tanveil District, not many blocks away from his apartment. He could make it, get safely behind armored doors. Then let them shoot at him all they liked.

As he ran, he could not help wondering who wanted to kill him? Why?

A disruptor fired again.

His lungs on fire, he ran, gasping, telling himself: *Just one block more. Just a few feet more.*

His building. Home. Safety.

His stomach wouldn't stop itching. He put his hand down, and it came up shiny, wet with blood.

He'd been hit. Gut-shot.

MacKenzie stared at his own blood with astonishment, feeling oddly giddy.

Shot down at my own front door.

How embarrassing.

It was not so much a terrible pain as a peculiar numbness, a lessening of his control over his own body as he began to drift down, down, down toward the pavement.

Peters had been right. MacKenzie would have liked to tell him that, but it was too late now.

As he passed out, Lyle MacKenzie told himself that in the next world, if any, he would pay more attention to the warnings of his friends.

Chapter Thirteen

Kayla stared at Yates Keller's still body, her senses whirling. What had she done? What had she done?

—I tried to warn you.

—Gods, Golias, I think I killed him.

—Find out, fast.

Keller was motionless, pale, and did not seem to be breathing. Kayla placed her hand against his neck and after a moment detected what she thought was a weak pulse. Not dead, no.

She attempted a mind probe but found his brain virtually inactive, dark and cold.

What have I done? she thought.

This is the revenge that I thought I wanted.

How stupid. How pointless.

The mindghost stirred within her.

—Kayla, you constantly confuse me. I thought you were eager to hurt him, to kill him if you could.

—So did I, Golias.

—You should be exulting.

—I don't feel any better for it. In fact, I think I feel worse.

—Why? You've vanquished your enemy. He lies there at your feet, doesn't he?

—And has this brought my parents back from the dead? Or restored all of the other people Keller harmed? Gods, I'm so tired of hurting people, Golias. Tired of hurting them, tired of killing them. This isn't the way I thought my life would be.

—None of us get many choices about who we are, Kayla. It's beggar's choice.

—You're wrong. We can make choices. Decide what we will or won't do. And I'm tired of violence, Golias. Tired of seeing my friends hurt or killed. Look at him lying there now. The only person who knows where Salome and the others are, and I may have killed him. Because I couldn't control myself.

—He's not dead.

—His mind is. And as far as I'm concerned, that's dead. Dead and gone.

—Are you certain that his brain is gone?

—I couldn't find anything when I probed him.

—Perhaps he can be revived at a medical facility.

—I hope you're right. But the nearest one is on St. Ilban, in Vardalia.

—It's a long walk.

—And I guess I've got to carry him again.

A sudden noise stopped her. Was it Natan, and the rest of Charon's Eyes, returning? No, that wasn't a cautious stealthy tread. More like the steady tramp of feet, walking casually but purposefully toward a goal.

Instinct told Kayla to hide and observe. She placed Keller in a small cave, out of sight, and went to investigate the source of the footsteps.

Two men and two women in matching pressure suits were opening the sealed entrance of a former cave dwelling. Inside were mining mechs and machinery, com boards and other controls. It looked like an ops center.

As Kayla watched, they began activating mechs. Lights blinked, boards beeped. From deep in the tunnels, Kayla could hear the hum of reactivated machinery. A steady thrumming began to course through the rock beneath her feet.

These people were reopening the mines! The mines that had shut down at Pelleas Karlson's demise. Who were they? Who had sent them and by what authority?

Kayla tried to probe them. To her frustration, she found that her mind powers were nearly exhausted, her probes losing focus, dissipating before they reached their targets.

Reduced to eavesdropping, she drew closer to the engineers as they chatted.

". . . bloody mechs need servicing."

"Why's he in such a lather to start up? We had to scramble to get here. Not even a full service detail."

"Don't ask questions. You'll live longer."

"That damned Merrick's no better than Karlson was, you ask me. New boss is same as old boss."

"Anybody's better than Karlson."

Kayla pulled away.

So, somehow Merrick had contrived to get access to the mines and was starting them up once again. That wily old bounty hunter was greedy, she knew that. And apparently, he was most greedy for mindstones. He'd managed to lay claim to the inactive stakes while nobody else was looking. He would come away with a fortune and considerable power. It was not a prospect that she greeted with any pleasure.

I never trusted Merrick the Blackbird, Kayla thought. *With good reason. But I could never pin anything on him, before. This knowledge might be useful. Very useful.*

She crept away from the engineers, retrieved Keller's inert body, and made for Styx Port. It was slow progress with her heavy burden, slowed even further by the constant need to check for anyone following her.

From stump to stalagmite, any cover, any shadow. It took her over an hour to reach the Port. She found it transformed.

The shuttle bay had become fully operational, brightly lit, mechs whirring and blinking. The engineers' arrival had reactivated the place.

A newly-arrived cruiser sat in its berth, blue lights flickering gently along its hull.

The engineers' ship. The only way out of Styx.

It had seen hard service, its surface pitted by tiny

meteors, but it was still spaceworthy. Kayla thought it was completely, utterly beautiful.

Briefly she wondered how Natan and his crew would take to this resurgence of mine activity. Not peacefully. Those engineers were in for an unpleasant surprise.

—Isn't it a bit late for such altruistic concerns?

—Shut up, Golias.

The shuttle bay was wide open. Once inside, Kayla secured the bay doors to prevent the engineers from following her and interfering.

A wall monitor with divided screen showed her a view of empty tunnels, the engineers working, another empty cave, and Natan, followed by two others in cowled robes, walking stealthily through the lower tunnels.

As Kayla watched, Natan reached toward one of his companions and grasped her hand.

The gesture was unmistably affectionate. The cowl fell back from the face of Natan's friend and Kayla stared in amazement. A blonde woman, of medium height, thin, with pale skin, a pointed chin, and pale green eyes. Natan's woman.

Her description could have matched that of Kayla's mother, Teresa Reed. But it wasn't her mother, had never been her mother at all. The ghostly woman whom the mine supervisors had spied and reported in their journals had been a member of Charon's Eyes, a fanatic, a stranger, all along.

I'm a fool, Kayla told herself. She felt the last flicker of obsessive hope die within her and with it the last tiny bit of her childhood.

Her mother was dead, long dead, and gone.

Stop clinging to ghosts, she told herself and turned away from the screens.

The engineer's shuttle set in dock, waiting for her, engines still ticking as they cooled.

Kayla pressed the access pad for the shuttle's air lock. There was no response. The cruiser was locked down tight. Kayla remembered a trick that Salome had once shown her using palm pads and pressure plates. In a matter of moments she had broken the lock.

Alarms began howling. She ignored them and made for the cruiser's ops center.

Ops, when she found it, was a small round room at the heart of the shuttle. Gratefully Kayla flung Yates Kaller down into a webcouch and applied herself to the serious business of stealing a ship.

It was a very old shuttle: the navboard was part of a communications complex that included a rudimentary knowbot. Kayla unlocked its controls and told the 'bot to begin the start-up sequence for ignition.

Next, the com board. Kill the sirens. She hooked up to the board's unbilicals and keyed it to the *Antimony*'s frequency. Boosting the transmission to full power, she called:

"Iger, can you hear me?"

Static blasted in her ears.

"Iger, this is Katie. Come in, please."

Was that a faint response or just more static?

"Iger, I'll rendezvous with you at point 0.27, as we agreed. Watch for an Alliance shuttle, registry number AC 1755."

She hoped he was still out there.

The shuttle's engines set up a vibrating hum as the ready lights came on.

Kayla notified the Port brain of imminent departure. The brain responded and the shuttle was seized suddenly by the magnetic grapples of the Port tracks.

With a shudder and clank the shuttle heaved out of its berth and began the slow ascent up and out of Styx's dead core, aiming for the planet doors and the freedom of space.

Kayla couldn't control her impatience. She had been too long below ground. When would she see the first star on her viewscreen? When would the enclosing rock give way to space and cold light? The stars, she had to see the stars.

How could she have lived here, spent all those years in the dark?

She tried the com board again. "Iger. Iger, come in. This is Katie."

Nothing but static.

Beside her, Yates Keller sat immobile in the webseat, eyes closed, mouth open. He looked dead.

Did this ship contain an autodoc? Kayla hadn't thought to look. There was no time now to leave the navboard and hunt up the autodoc. Yates would have to wait.

—You may be losing the only chance you have of finding your friends.

—Golias, there's only one of me. I can either see to his medical needs or get us out of here. And every second I delay means that those engineers might find a way of stopping me. Which means that I definitely won't find Salome and the others.

Her attention was caught by a glimmer of light, of movement, on the viewscreen. Was it the planet doors? Yes. They were opening slowly, showing her a thin slice of the waiting universe. *Hurry,* she thought. Her pulse pounded at the sight of the familiar stars of the local galaxies.

As the shuttle cleared the doors, Kayla triggered full power. The craft moved quickly out and beyond the gravity well of the planet, putting Styx safely behind them.

And there, on the starboard, a small reddish star moving swiftly, resolving itself into a cruiser. Kayla smiled at the familiar shape: the *Antimony,* matching her speed. Iger had heard her. He had come.

The two ships performed a neat pas de deux, maneuvering deftly for transfer from one to the other. Before she knew it, Kayla was safely aboard the *Antimony,* and the shuttle was on its way back to Styx via autopilot.

Iger's smile nearly split his face as she entered the

Antimony's air lock, but it faded as he saw the body that Kayla was carrying. "What the hell?"

"It's Yates Keller," she said. "I've nearly killed him, Iger. We've got to get him hooked up to an autodoc."

"But I thought you wanted to kill him." Iger took Keller's limp body from her and hefted it easily. "Did you find out where Salome and the others are?"

"No, dammit. That's why I'm trying so hard to keep him alive. Help me get him onto a gelcouch."

The trodes from the autodoc went around Keller's head, chest, and wrists. He lay on the gelbed with eyes half-open, as pale and silent as a corpse.

The autodoc chuttered and clacked.

"Doesn't look good," Iger said after a minute. "No alpha activity registering at all."

"Give it a chance to check him over."

Kayla stood by, watching nervously as the autodoc checked and rechecked Yates Keller's mind and body. "Hmmm. There was a flash there, onscreen, for just a moment."

"A power surge."

"It could have been brain activity."

"Maybe." Iger's voice was soft. She knew he was being kind. And again she was struck by the incongruity of hoping that her worst enemy was still alive. Looking into Iger's blue eyes, she saw that he understood that, too.

"Gods, Iger, distract me, tell me something else."

"Third Child is okay. Kind of cranky, but I think that's normal—if anything is normal about her situation."

"I'll go see her." Without a backward glance for the body on the gelcouch Kayla strode from the room.

She was halfway to Third Child's quarters when the hallway pulsed and the walls began to move.

"What?" Kayla grabbed at a wall hold only to have it shimmer and eel away from her, squeaking.

The air was liquid, running yellow and green through the corridor.

The floor melted and re-formed into shards of ice.

"Gods!"

—I don't like this, Kayla. Not at all.

—Think that I do, Golias?

—Well, do something about it!

The walls ruptured, and silvery funnels of steam slithered through the breaches and spun their way down the hall.

A headless torso came shooting past in pursuit of a bambera herd. It caught one of the animals, held it as it wriggled wildly, and snatched off the head. Triumphant, it placed the bambera head upon its own empty shoulders.

Kayla froze, staring at the galloping nightmare. "What in the name of all gods—?"

Pink and red jellyfish floated down the corridor, meowing like cats.

It all has a terribly familiar feel to it, Kayla thought.

The hallway pulsed yet again.

She began running for Third Child's room.

"Third Child!" she cried. "Third Child, are you all right? Answer me!"

She dodged a blue three-headed dog that materialized out of thin air, and jumped over a small volcano erupting with sulphurous mud and bubbles.

"Third Child!" Kayla skidded through the door and found the dalkoi stretched out on its cot, eyes half-lidded. "What's going on? Have you been drinking choba ale again?"

For answer, the dalkoi burped. A delicate six-legged bambera with purple wings flew across the room and out the wall. The dalkoi watched it for a moment and moaned gently.

"God's Eyes," Kayla said, understanding flooding her. "You're not drunk. You're sick, aren't you? And that's why you're generating these phantasms."

—Brilliant deduction, Kayla.

—Shut up, Golias. "I'd recognize these hallucinations anywhere," she told the dalkoi. "They're just like the ones you set off in Vardalia when you absorbed too many mindstones."

Third Child chirped weakly in apparent agreement.

The wall com came to life. "Katie?" Iger said. "Have you reached Third Child yet?"

"I'm with her now. She's the source of these crazy hallucinations."

"I'm relieved to know it's not me going spacebatty. Tell her to knock it off. I can't plot course and deal with firesnakes coming out of the navboard."

"I don't think she has any control over it. I think she's sick to her stomach."

"Wonderful."

"I'll try to get some soup into her."

"Try anything, but get her shut down."

Kayla raced for the galley, grabbed and triggered a self-heating soup pack, and was back by Third Child's side in moments. "Try some of this."

The dalkoi turned away from the steaming packet.

"Too hot?"

Kayla waited until the soup had cooled and offered it again. "You should eat something."

Still Third Child refused to touch the soup. She lay belching upon her cot, looking miserable as fantastic beasts swam through the air and awful monsters erupted from the walls and floor.

When Kayla attempted to address the dalkoi in mindspeech, she refused to answer.

Meanwhile the walls moved in and out, lightning flashed from the ceiling, and firetrees dripped flaming blossoms that melted the floorplates.

The hallucinations were harmless. But they could keep Iger from charting a safe course. The *Antimony* was stuck in orbit around Styx, no closer to Vardalia and medical help for Keller. No closer to finding Salome, Rab, and Arsobades.

Something had to be done.

Kayla hit the wall com. "Iger, get down here."

"Are you nuts? I'm still trying to plot a course."

"Well, put it on autopilot. I need you here, now. Move it!"

He was there in a heartbeat, blue eyes filled with concern. "Mind telling me what is so all-bloody urgent?"

"Link with me."

"Now?"

"Right now."

A squad of screaming demon things with human faces and hoofed feet raced past the door.

"We've got to get through to Third Child somehow and try to stop this."

Iger gave her a disgusted look.

She knew how little he enjoyed mind-to-mind contact.

In a moment of desperate need she had discovered Iger's nascent mindpower. He was too weak an empath to utilize his powers on his own. But he heartily disliked having them enhanced any place other than in bed.

And now there was the presence of Golias to factor into the mix. Iger would be furious that the mindghost had survived. But there was no time for niceties.

She shrugged an apology and linked with Iger on their private mode, feeling him shudder at the intimate contact.

—*Ready?*

—*As ready as I'll ever be.*

With him she plunged into Third Child's consciousness. It was like sliding down a long, curving slope. Suddenly they were looking at a strange world filled with an abundance of peculiar things. Two of those things were tall bipeds, one with long yellow hair pulled back in a tail, the other with a cap of short red hair. It took a moment to realize that they were looking at themselves through Third Child's eyes.

—*I'm getting dizzy,* Iger told Kayla.

Golias spoke up. —*Me, too.*

Iger reacted to the mindghost's presence exactly as Kayla had expected. —*What the hell? He's not back, is he? I don't want to be linked to him, too, Katie.*

Kayla had no time for petty rivalries and squeamishness. —*Shut up, both of you! I'm busy.*

That bright peach-toned spot over there, that was Third Child's conscious mind. But close to it was a small yellow sphere. What was that?

As they bore down upon it, it seemed to spin in circles, emanating fear.

And Kayla realized what they were seeing.

—*That's the fetus. Third Child's child. She really is*

pregnant after all. Iger, Golias, it's terrified. We've got to comfort it, help it somehow.

It was Golias who asked: —*How in the universe do you reassure an alien fetus?*

Love, Kayla thought. —*We've got to surround it with love. Tell it we care about it.*

—*Great,* Iger said.

—*You first,* urged Golias.

Kayla centered herself, breathed deeply, and thought: —*We love you, baby.*

She felt slightly ridiculous, but she vanquished that thought and intensified the reassuring message. —*Love. You're part of us. There's nothing to fear. All is well.*

She sent those thoughts, and wordless emanations of warm emotion, at the tiny sprite.

Haltingly, Iger joined in.

—*Love, love, love.*

A ghostly tendril from Golias joined them.

—*All is well.*

The fetus' oscillations began to slacken.

Kayla concentrated on the tiny thing, sensing that as it calmed, Third Child was also becoming calmer.

—*Love. Calm. Love.*

The fetus grew languid now, stilling all frantic motion. It seemed to expand slightly, sighing, as its color deepened to a soft peach that nearly matched that of its mother.

—*Love.*

The fetus pulsed gently, in-out-in, in-out-in, firmly in rhythm with Third Child's heartbeat.

—That's better.

In-out-in.

Child and mother were breathing easily, in sync. Kayla watched for a moment longer, then decided that it was safe for her and Iger to disengage.

Up the winding path and out into the real world.

Shorn of their mindlink, Kayla and Iger stared at one another in amazement.

"I don't believe that," Iger said. His relief was palpable, both for himself and the dalkoi.

"I'm not sure I believe it either." Had they really communicated with Third Child's unborn child, Kayla wondered, or had that been just another hallucination? Real, she decided. Definitely real.

The dalkoi was curled on her bunk, eyes closed, breathing slowly. She appeared to be fast asleep.

"C'mon," Iger whispered, indicating the door.

Together they tiptoed back to ops. The floor stayed where it was and the walls never once budged along the way.

Gratefully Kayla sank into her webseat. "Iger, let's go to Vardalia before anything else happens."

Chapter Fourteen

St. Ilban was a tiny golden glimmer, a jewel set at the mid-curve of purple Xenobe's belly.

Under Iger's steady hand, *Antimony* shot smoothly past the moonlet's orbital buoys and made for port.

Kayla punched in the com code for Vardalia Port. "Vardalia, this is the light cruiser *Antimony,* registry TS 275959, requesting docking assignment.

"*Antimony,*" said a toneless voice. "We comp your registry. Who's the captain?"

"Kate N. Shadow." Kayla waited for the warmth of the recognition to spread through the speaker's voice. Instead, she heard static, and then, "*Antimony,* we confirm your trajectory. Berth 71–A is open. Vardalia Port out."

"Odd," Kayla said. "I don't recognize that voice. I thought we left Mepal Tarlinger in charge."

"Maybe she's off-shift," Iger said. "You can't know everybody in Vardalia Port communications."

The *Antimony* made berth easily. Down-station

transport was waiting. With Yates Keller stretched between them on a null-g pallet, Kayla and Iger left the ship and made their way from the shuttle bay into the port's main processing center. Kayla was surprised to see a security checkpoint just inside the main doors. What was going on here?

An officious-looking man in a gray and black jacket held out his hand and rasped, "ID, please."

Kayla stared at him in amazement. "What do you mean? We cleared port authority. What the hell is this?"

His eyes were dark and hostile. "Which part of the request don't you understand? ID? Please?"

"When was this policy started?"

"What does that matter? You want into Vardalia, you show me some ID, fast."

Before she could protest, Iger leaned over her shoulder and flashed their holostats. "Good enough?"

The official grunted. "Fine. What about that guy in the null-g stretcher?"

"He's crew," Kayla said quickly.

"I don't see anything about crew in these stats."

"Are you accusing me of lying?" Kayla rested her hand on the top of her disruptor holster, knowing that the gesture wouldn't go unnoticed. "You can see he's in need of medical assistance. Your delaying us here may be grounds for later action."

The man shrugged and waved them through.

At the hospital there were more checkpoints and more demands for holostats. They left Keller in the hands of two worried-looking interns.

"I want to call Mac," Kayla said.

A purple-striped com kiosk stood near the door in the hospital lobby. Kayla punched in Lyle MacKenzie's office com code.

The screen rolled through a series of orange numerals before fixing on the sequence that Kayla had given it. The code froze onscreen, pulsing gently.

"That's odd," Kayla said. "It's not going through."

"Maybe Mac took the day off."

"I'll try him at home."

She dialed the code. Again, the numerals froze onscreen. Again, that hypnotic, frustrating pulse.

Kayla hung up the headpiece. "I don't like this, not in the slightest. It feels wrong. Let's get over to the Crystal Palace on the double."

Outside the hospital they found their path blocked by a group of ragged men and women. There was much screaming and cursing, all of it directed at two men in blue stretchsuits who were walking quickly across the street.

"Bastards! Sold us out to the police, didn't you?"

"Where's the salt? Where're you hiding it?"

The two men paused, conferred, and, in sync, pulled out disruptors.

"Get down," Iger yelled.

But Kayla had already seen the glint of weapons and ducked for cover.

ZZZat!!

ZZZaaZZat!!

One of the men in blue cursed and grabbed his arm. His companion fired furiously.

A woman screamed and beside her, a man fell over and stayed spread-eagled upon the pavement.

ZZatat!

The gunfight began to spread along the street. People were running for cover, crying out, returning fire. Others lay ominously still as dark puddles spread beneath them.

"Has this entire city gone crazy?" Iger said.

Kayla kept her hand on her gun and said, "Until we talk to Mac, we won't know what's been happening."

Slowly they crawled away from the fracas, around a corner, and into the relative quiet of another street.

It wasn't an easy journey to the Crystal Palace.

They circled past street fights, burning skimmers, and piles of rotting garbage. Zigged through narrow passageways, zagged past dark corners.

Everywhere they went Kayla and Iger saw people in turmoil, fighting, shooting, shouting at one another. Vardalia was a city run amok.

At the juncture of the Musician's District and the Beggar's Quarter a group of ragged, tough-looking folk came like shadows out of the doorways and back alleys to block their way.

Kayla's disruptor was in her hand. She fired once, deliberately missing them.

"The next shot will take out at least three of you," she said loudly. "Is it worth it?"

There was a break in the crowd. Kayla made for it with Iger right behind her.

A few men gave half-hearted chase but quickly abandoned the effort.

"I'm glad we left Third Child on the ship!" Iger panted.

"Just shut up and run."

—Perhaps you should find a safe place and attempt to contact your friend again.

—Golias, would you care to show me a safe place?

—I see your point.

They passed through a district where the side streets were all blocked and armed citizens patrolled the barricades.

"And just where do you think you're going?" The voice was high, a rasping soprano. The speaker stood before them, legs planted firmly. She was a woman of about fifty, gray-haired and flinty-eyed, wearing a black stretchsuit. She held a magnum disruptor and had another strapped to her back. Three well-muscled men stood at her side, also holding disruptors. All of the weapons were trained on Kayla and Iger.

"Spacers, from the look of you," the woman said. "Merrick will pay well for your weapons."

"Merrick?" Kayla said. "Merrick the Blackbird?"

The woman squinted. "You know of any other?"

"I should have known he was behind this, that bastard."

A bit of the woman's self-assurance chipped off. "You know Merrick well?"

"Know him? I'm Kate Shadow. I gave him his job. Talk about a bad idea."

The woman stared, obviously trying to decide whether or not to believe her.

One of her companions, a balding, beefy man, leaned closer. "You're Kate Shadow?"

"Same."

"Merrick said that if you showed up we were to bring you to him immediately."

"Bring me?" Kayla's temper began to get the better of her. "I can get there just fine under my own power, thank you. In fact, that's precisely where we were headed when you people got in our way."

The smallest of the men, a wiry fellow with tattooed cheeks, nodded at her. "Kate, I was with you aboard the *Admiral Lovejoy*. I won't ever forget what you did for us. How you freed us. Gave us all another chance."

Kayla saw the opening and lunged for it. "It's good to see you, friend. None of us will forget the *Lovejoy*, will we? Bad times and plenty of them. But we survived. And we've got a lot of work ahead of us here."

The flint-eyed woman's grip on her disruptor wavered. "But I thought—"

Kayla reached out and gently pushed the gun down. "Would you act as our escort to the Palace? It's pretty dangerous on these streets."

The woman frowned, then shrugged. "What the hell." She nodded sharply and the men with her lowered their guns, too. "Merrick never pays on time anyway."

"Hey!" the thin, tattooed War Minstrel called to some other armed residents across the street. "Hey, it's Kate Shadow here. She's come back. She didn't desert us after all!"

There were disbelieving looks as people began to wander over, staring hard at her.

"That's right," Kayla said, raising her voice. She stepped forward so that more of the crowd could see her. "It's good to greet so many old comrades. I'm back to help put Vardalia into shape. Who'll come with me to the Crystal Palace? Who'll help me make the streets safe again?"

"Kate?" somebody cried. "Kate Shadow's back? I thought she was gone for good."

"Let me see her! I don't believe it."

"Katie's come back to clean this place up."

"Now we'll see some action."

As the word spread, more came running, anxious to believe, to join, to follow her once more.

"Kate N. Shadow," they said. "We'll follow her anywhere. We'll do anything she says. She's one of us. Didn't she set us free? Didn't she lead us out of the dark?"

As Kayla moved through the streets with Iger at her side and an ever-growing group of followers, she heard the company behind her begin to sing:

"Katie saved us. Katie loves us. Katie, our darling, our favorite, our own.
She killed seven men with her bare hands alone.
Took us from prison and led us to freedom,
Katie, our Katie
Our mother. Our home.
Give us a target, give us a quest,
Some way that we can return the favor.
Katie, who saved us. Katie, who loves us, who freed us,
Our darling, our leader, our own."

It was the old War Minstrel fighting song, the one that Arsobades had composed for her.

The crowd sang through it twice, and when that song died away, they began to chant a familiar refrain:

"Free Trade forever, Free Traders, free!
Free Trade forever, Free Traders, free!"

Kayla felt a lump growing in her throat. She felt Arsobades marching beside her, and Rab and Salome as well.

I'll find you, old friends, she vowed. *I'll find you and set you free, I promise.*

When the shots rang out, Kayla thought at first that it was more high spirits, that her supporters were shooting into the sky. But the crowd began screaming and scattered. Iger grabbed Kayla, knocking her to the ground.

"Ow! What the hell?"

The very people who had pulled guns on her minutes before were now defending her, encircling her and shielding her with their own bodies.

"Stop shooting!" shouted a short, helmeted man in a gray and gold armored stretchsuit. He pointed an enormous laser rifle at the heart of the group. "Police! Put down your weapons. We're here to protect Kate Shadow!"

"Yeah?" rasped the man with tattooed cheeks. "Well, maybe we're already protecting her."

"Is that right? More like capturing her, from the looks of things."

"Bullshit! You work for the government. You were trying to kill her. And us."

The man in armor held up his hand. "No. No, you've got to believe me. We want her safe just as much as you do."

Kayla stood up, brushing herself off. "I believe

you, officer. But tell me why the Police Minister sent out an entire battalion of bodyguards. What's happening here? Civil War?"

"Close to it." The cop nodded. "I'm Lieutenant Commander Sherno, Ms. Shadow. You'd better come with us."

Angry voices protested:

"Screw off, Kate's with us."

"Damned cops."

"All they're good for is busting up bars."

"There's more of us than them. Let's take their guns! Show them all who's in charge."

"Wait!" Kayla held up her hands. "No more fighting. Let's all go to the Crystal Palace. Together." She waited until she saw agreement on the faces in the crowd.

Lt. Commander Sherno gave her an uneasy look.

"Together," she said sharply, and began walking, tugging Iger along with her.

The crowd fell in behind, police and War Minstrels mixing. There was some shoving, some shouting, but the progression to the Crystal Palace was relatively peaceful.

The guards at the Palace put an end to that.

Standing shoulder to shoulder they nearly encircled the huge crystal structure. Each of them held a huge magnum disruptor aimed directly at the crowd. Their faces were covered by reflective shields. The effect was strange and frightening: an army of mechs with mirrors for faces.

We could lose it right here, Kayla worried. *One shot and we're done for, every single one of us. Mass riot, war, suicide. Whatever you call it. Finished.*

Within her the mindghost Golias stirred uneasily. —*I suggest that you allow somebody else to stand at the head of the line—or even better, several people.*

—*I can't afford to show fear, Golias. It would undo every person here.*

—*You're taking a terrible chance.*

—*It's not the first time, is it?*

She took a deep breath. "I'm Kate Shadow and I want to see Lyle MacKenzie."

There was no response save that a few of the disruptors were raised even higher.

"Move aside, I say!"

The guards massed now, training their weapons directly upon her.

There was the sound of a dozen disruptors being clicked into maximum phase readiness. The police weren't accustomed to facing down an elite guard.

Lt. Commander Sherno stepped out of the shadows, moving in front of Kayla, motioning her to get back.

"Go on," she said. "Take control of the guards."

"I'm afraid I can't do that."

"What do you mean? Aren't they part of the police force and subordinate to you?"

Sherno shook his head grimly. "Private guards. Merrick hired them."

"Damn." She took a step forward and addressed the guards. "If Mac isn't here, then I want to see whoever is in charge. Is Merrick the Blackbird here? Is he the one that wants my blood on his hands? My blood and the blood of all these people? Does he?"

A public address system came to life and Kayla heard the familiar basso rumble of Merrick's voice. "You're the one who brought the killing mob here, Kate. I'm merely defending myself against a riot, a riot that you're leading."

"Merrick, show yourself!"

"I don't think so."

"If you don't come out, I'll sure as hell come in." She eyed the mirror-faced troopers and wondered how many of them she could mind squeeze before they got her.

A gusty sigh resounded through the plaza. The voice, when it spoke again, was deeper, more rasping. "You always were a stubborn girl, Katie."

"It's gotten worse, Merrick, now that I'm a woman. Call off your troops. I've got the police with me. Your guards might be able to take me, might take out a few of us. But some will get through, get into the palace. And they'll be looking for you, Merrick. Either show your face or find a good hiding place."

Iger gave her an approving nod.

The PA remained silent.

Behind Kayla, the crowd rumbled ominously.

Suddenly the ranks of mirror-faced guards broke open as though hinged. At their middle stood Merrick the Blackbird, scowling. His dark robes flowed out behind him like wings. "All right," he said. "I'm here."

Kayla pointed her finger at him. "Damn you," she cried. "Where's Lyle MacKenzie?"

Chapter Fifteen

"MacKenzie is under my protection," Merrick said smoothly. "He's recovering from a nasty disruptor wound."

At that, some of the police in the crowd stirred and Kayla heard mocking whispers.

"Shot? Mac was shot?" Kayla's face and voice were ice cold, stone hard. "How did that happen?"

"We don't know."

"Ms. Shadow," Lt. Commander Sherno said quietly. "Don't believe him. You've flushed out the Blackbird. Let's take him while we've got him standing in front of us."

"No," she said, sotto voce. "I don't believe that bastard either. But I can't just shoot him down in cold blood."

Merrick gave a mocking bow that sent his robes swinging. "Please don't stand out here in the open air. Come inside and we'll talk. Have tea."

Kayla felt a memory stir within her: a day years

ago when Merrick had been a bounty hunter intent on selling her to the Keller family on Styx for a handsome price. For a moment she was back there, hating him. Then the moment passed, the memory faded. "Free tea, Merrick? And will I wake up in the hold of another prison ship?" Her tone was light, but her message was unmistakable: I don't trust you, Blackbird.

Merrick's dark eyes glinted with anger. "Bring your own guards if it'll make you feel better."

"Fine." She turned to the woman who had first apprehended her and said, "You keep order here while I'm inside. If I'm not back in half an hour, come in shooting."

"Yes'm."

Turning to Iger and Lt. Commander Sherno, she said, "C'mon. Let's go have tea with the Blackbird."

* * *

Kayla saw that Merrick's living quarters glittered with newly-rubbed richness, its mosaics buffed and scrubbed, its tapestries splendid with jewel-toned glory.

"This all looks familiar," she said. "*Very* familiar. Weren't these once Karlson's room?"

The Blackbird made no reply, merely stood glowering by the main fireplace, and lit up a smoke stick.

"Yes, I'm sure of it." She looked toward the center

of the wall for the familiar holoportrait of the late prime minister. It was gone. In its place was a portrait of Merrick. The self-satisfied smile on the holoimage made Kayla want to smash it.

A familiar figure sat upon burgundy pillows, resplendent in golden bambera leathers and a velvet cloak. Dark glossy hair, golden skin, and dark eyes shaded by lids with an epicanthic fold. He rose, grinning, and held out his arms.

"Kate."

She recoiled. "You?" Beside her Iger muttered a disgusted curse.

It was Cristobal, dressed as though he were going to a formal dinner.

"What the hell are you doing here?" she said.

He clutched his chest as though wounded. "Katie," he cried. "Is that how you greet your old comrade-in-arms?" In two steps he was at her side, shoving Iger back, attempting to embrace her.

Kayla stiff-armed him, hard, and gave him a sour look. "Old betrayer, you mean. I thought you were dead, Cristobal. What asteroid did you crawl out from under?"

Cristobal tried to grab her again and this time it took an elbow in his stomach to discourage him.

"Ow!"

He pulled back, rubbing his abdomen and staring at her with what looked like real dismay.

"I thought you were dead, traitor. At least I'd

hoped that you'd perished in that Alliance firestorm you called down on us. How did you get here? And why are you with Merrick?"

Cristobal opened his mouth to reply.

"It's a long story," Merrick rumbled, stepping in. "Suffice it to say that our mutual friend here ducked out when the Three Systems Alliance troops engaged ours, and saved his own precious hide in the process."

"As usual," Kayla said. She paused and stared at Cristobal. Once he had claimed to know where Salome and the others had been taken. A mindprobe might yield their location.

She aimed a narrow probe at her former coleader. What she found shocked her.

His mind seemed to be almost as empty as that of Yates Keller. Riddled with wormholes, hollowed out by mindsalt. Cristobal had become a mindsalt addict. What was left of his personality was tremendously paranoid and easily influenced by suggestion. No wonder he was aligned with Merrick. Who else could he run to?

She wouldn't find her friends here.

Shuddering, Kayla withdrew her probe. She needed a moment to regain her composure and gazed around the room, taking in the rich ornaments, the tapestries, and glittering decanters. "Well, Merrick," she said. "It looks like you didn't lose any time, did you? Looted at least half of the palace, I see. And probably half of the city as well."

Merrick said nothing, but a muscle in his jaw worked.

Kayla turned on him, smiling a feral smile. "Where's Mac?" Her tone was deceptively light.

"In a safe house on Mergui Boulevard," said the Blackbird. "It's a big blue building on a corner lot. I'll provide an escort there for you."

"Thanks, but I've got my own." Kayla gave Iger the high sign and he was on his feet in a moment. "It shouldn't be too difficult to find a big blue building."

Merrick was on his feet. "But we haven't had tea yet." He looked genuinely insulted.

"I'd love to have some. But I didn't bring my poison-detector." She nodded and Lt. Commander Sherno rose as well.

As the door Kayla paused, leaned back in, and said, "Don't worry, Merrick, we'll be in touch. Count on it."

* * *

"Katie!" Lyle MacKenzie cried. "Gods, but you're the best thing I've laid eyes upon in days."

He was thin and pale, with dark half-moons under each eye. His gingery hair lay flat and slick against his skull and his wispy beard looked worse than usual. But he was smiling, sitting up in bed, and he eagerly waved her to his bedside.

"Didn't I say to everybody that you'd be back, Katie? Now tell me all about it, don't leave out a bit. How did you settle with that bastard Yates Keller? Where are Salome and all the rest? I can't wait to see them."

Kayla bit her lip. MacKenzie presumed that she had succeeded in finding his friends and that made what she had to tell him even more difficult. "Mac, I still don't know where Salome, Rab, and Arsobades are."

MacKenzie's smile faltered. "Didn't you meet Keller?"

"Oh, I met him, all right. And nearly killed him. He's in a hospital here in Vardalia."

"In Vardalia? How'd he get here?"

"Iger and I brought him." MacKenzie's stare was beginning to make her feel uncomfortable.

"Brought him? Your old enemy?"

"Mac, I almost killed him."

"Before he told you where your friends were?" His eyes bored into her.

"I know it was stupid, Mac. Spare me the lecture and tell me how you got hurt."

He gave her a wry smile. "We may be partners in stupidity, Katie. Darius Peters warned me to cover my back, but I laughed off the warning. I'm not laughing now, I can tell you that."

"Any idea who did it?"

MacKenzie shrugged, wincing from the motion. "I've got my suspicions. Mindsalt dealers. Peters has been hitting them pretty hard, and with my blessing. So they got together and decided to hit me back is my guess." He nodded toward Lt. Commander Sherno. "If he hadn't come along and found me bleeding to death on my own doorstep, we wouldn't be having this conversation. He hustled me off to the hospital, and had his officers guard my door."

Sherno smiled in embarrassed pleasure. "Just part of my job. Minister Peters told me to keep an eye on him. Wish I'd gotten there a minute sooner, though."

"It's enough that you didn't get there a minute later. I was nearly done for."

Kayla squeezed MacKenzie's arm. "It's good to see you, Mac. We'll let you rest. I've got to get back to check on Keller." She paused. "Iger, will you stay with him?"

"Sure." He settled into a webseat. "I'll sing Mac to sleep. Tell him dalkoi bedtime stories. Just call me from the hospital, will you?"

She nodded.

"It'll be business as usual," MacKenzie said happily, oblivious to their byplay. "Now that you're back we'll set things to rights, Katie."

"Sure we will, Mac. Sleep now."

His eyes closed. Like an obedient child, he was asleep before she left the room.

"How bad is he?" she asked Sherno.

"It was a close call," said the lieutenant. "Very close. But he's mending. Slowly. I just hope we can keep him safe."

Kayla stared at him in surprise. "Things have gotten that bad here?"

"You were out on the streets," Sherno said. "You saw how it is."

"What in God's Eyes happened?"

"When my boss tried to shut down the mindsalt trade, all hell broke loose. Death threats, counterthreats, gang warfare. This city is wide open and up for grabs—and the Three Systems Alliance with it."

"Mindsalt," Kayla said, and the word was a curse. "I wish I'd never heard of it."

"Minister Peters agrees. And he wants to see you."

Kayla nodded. "Fine. When?"

"Now."

"You said something earlier about not trusting what Merrick told me?"

"Better let my boss explain it to you."

"Then lead on."

* * *

Darius Peters greeted Kayla from behind a massive, scarred desk. He looked as if he hadn't slept in days. His wide face was weary and his eyes were heavy-lidded.

"You've returned at a most opportune time," he said. "You might just save your friend Lyle MacKenzie's life."

"Me? How?"

"By getting him out of Merrick's reach."

"Merrick shot him?"

"Had him shot."

"What? Do you have proof?"

Grimly, Peters shook his head. "No, I can't prove a thing. But I'm certain of it. And I can't protect MacKenzie constantly. He's a good man, but he's too honest, too trusting."

Kayla stared at the man. "Why would the Blackbird want to have MacKenzie killed?"

"He thinks that MacKenzie's behind the squeeze on mindsalt and stones, that if he gets rid of him the pressure will stop and he'll have the entire field to himself. He doesn't realize that I convinced Mac to let me go after the mindsalt trade in the first place. And I'll still be here." He paused. "But I can't give Mac the protection he deserves. You can."

"Me? Where do you propose that I stash Mac?"

"On your ship."

"The *Antimony*?"

"Merrick can't have somebody killed when he doesn't know where he is."

"But surely he'll have spies posted at the port."

"We can arrange a diversion. Besides, as I understand it, you aren't exactly at a loss for resources."

"You mean my empathic powers?"

"Exactly."

"They're not always reliable."

"You'll have an armed escort. And I've seen how you handle yourself, Kate. I think Mac will be safer with you than with an entire police battalion."

"I wish that were true. But I can't babysit Mac. Not now. I've got friends who are in worse trouble than he is. They're my priority. Besides, he looks too fragile to move."

Peters sighed heavily. "I hate to admit it, but you're right. Will you come back for Mac?"

"When I can."

"I hope that's soon. Otherwise, he might not be here."

"I hope you're wrong," Kayla said. "I'll give you descriptions of the people I'm looking for. Perhaps you'll find them first. I'm desperate, Peters. I'll take any help I can get."

"Fair enough. Give the particulars to Lt. Commander Sherno." He stared her in the eye. "You don't have much time. You can see what's happening on the streets now. Soon we're going to have to impose martial law, which will put us right up against Merrick's forces. We're heading toward real bloodshed here."

Kayla thought of the name Charon's Eyes had

called her. Sister Blood. Of how tired she was of the hurting and the killing. "Gods," she said fervently, "I hope you're wrong."

"Me, too. But I've got to ask you to keep yourself visible in Vardalia. You can help keep order. I saw that mob outside. The people flock to you."

"I'm not an administrator."

"Bull. You ran a revolution, didn't you? Now let's see how you handle peacetime."

"It doesn't look very peaceful out there to me."

"Make your presence felt. Let the people see you. Shove Merrick back into his place."

"I don't have time for that now."

"Don't you care about Vardalia?"

Stung, Kayla said, "You sound like you'd like to run things, Minister Peters. Why don't you just grab power?"

Instead of snarling back at her as she expected, he gave her a slow smile. "Some people I know think that I should." A memory lingered in his eyes for a moment then was gone. "But I don't want it. I've got enough to handle as it is."

"I can see that."

"If I try to locate your friends, will you do your part and try to keep Merrick in his place?"

"While I'm here."

"Fair enough."

"Peters, you're a good man," Kayla said. "I'll do what I can." She stood. "But right now I'm heading for the hospital, to see an old enemy and pray for his health."

* * *

A medic met her at the door to Keller's room. His eyes above the half-mask were somber.

"Tell me," she said.

"That's Yates Keller, isn't it?" the medic asked. "He used to run Vardalia."

"Not anymore," said Kayla.

The medic nodded. "Or ever."

"What are you saying?"

"I'm sorry. We can't resuscitate him."

The words didn't quite make sense. Kayla blinked and said, "You mean that he's in a coma?"

"Not exactly. We can keep the body alive indefinitely for all the good that'll do. But there's absolutely no neural activity, not a trace. He's brain dead."

"You're certain?"

"Yes."

She nodded slowly, taking it in. She could almost—almost—comprehend the situation. But her brain had slowed, her mind refused to wrap itself around this new and awful truth. "Can I be alone with him?"

The medic nodded understandingly, misunderstanding everything. "Of course."

The door was closed, and she sat down beside the still body of Yates Keller.

Brain dead. She couldn't accept it. The medic had to be wrong. Had to be.

Kayla gathered every bit of her mental energy, honed and focused it until it was needle thin, and aimed it for the deepest recesses of Keller's mind. It went in swift as an arrow, smooth as a laser scalpel.

—Yates? Yates, can you hear me?

Silence.

—Yates?

Kayla couldn't detect even the slightest hint of cognition, neither a mind signature nor the manic babble, static, and stutter of the subconscious.

Not even the barest subvocalized whisper ghosted through the darkness. There was nothing, nothing but a black and empty pit, bottomless, in which she flew blind.

—Yates? Yates, you can't be gone. Answer me. Answer me, please.

Her own mindvoice became a mocking echo, bouncing back at her in the gloom.

Please, please, please.

—YATES, DAMN YOU!

Before the mindshout had completely died away, Kayla fled the empty vault that had contained Yates Keller. She stared at the closed pale face, knowing that the heart still pumped, the lungs still breathed. She had not managed to damage his autonomic nervous system. But only the shell, his physical body, survived. The brain was gone.

Self-loathing cut through Kayla, sharp-edged and nauseating. Her recklessness had condemned Salome, Rab, and Arsobades to death. The fanatics of Charon's Eyes were right, she was indeed Sister Blood: she destroyed whatever she touched.

Chapter Sixteen

The com kiosk was just down the hall. Kayla punched in the code for Lyle MacKenzie's safe house, heard it ring and ring again. Then Iger's face, flattened and expanded, was staring at her from the kiosk screen.

"Well?" he said.

"No good. Keller's brain dead."

"Katie, I'm sorry." Iger's eyes were filled with an emotion—pity?—which infuriated her.

"I don't want your sympathy, Iger. I want to save Salome, Rab, and Arsobades. Only I'm not going to be able to do that. Do you understand, Iger? Do you? Because of me, they're going to die. And that's what happens to whoever comes near me."

"Katie, you're talking crazy."

"Get away, Iger. I'm poison, and you'll be next."

Iger rolled his eyes up and made an exasperated sound.

Kayla cut the connection.

The com kiosk began chiming for her attention, but she stormed away from it and raced down the corridor, nearly upending a cleaning mech in her path.

—Kayla, wait.

She ignored the mindghost's entreaty. She would get back to the port, get on the *Antimony*, and go lose herself in jumpspace. Or ram the ship into an asteroid. No, a supernova.

—Kayla, there's one other option.

—Don't be a fool, Golias! There's nothing left of Keller, nothing at all. Do you expect me to waste more time probing a dead mind while my friends are dying because of me?

—Calm yourself. There's still a chance. Let's go back to Keller's room. I have an idea.

—All right. I'll try anything.

Keller was a pale corpselike figure covered by blue bedclothes, his chest slowly rising and falling with each almost-imperceptible breath.

—Probe him again.

—But, Golias, I told you . . .

—Just do it, will you?

A part of Kayla wondered why she was acquiescing. But she was desperate, and that desperation gave her strength as she formed another probe, readied it, and, with Golias' urging, plunged back into the empty mind of Yates Keller.

Again she was suspended in darkness, in silence, reliving the awfulness of what she had done.

—*See? I told you, there's nothing here, just like before.*

The mindghost said nothing.

With a silent curse, Kayla pulled out of Keller.

The room was the same. Keller lay in bed as be-ore, breathing slowly.

Then, a twitch of his face.

His eyelids fluttered.

Opened.

Keller sat up in bed and looked at her.

"Oh, no," Kayla said. "I don't belive this. It's sim-ly not possible."

The mouth worked, lips quivering, but no sound ame out. The eyes unfocused, closed, opened again.

"More things possible than you think," Keller said. he words were slurred, the voice pitched oddly.

Terror struck at Kayla's soul.

"Yates? Yates, that is you, isn't it?"

Again the mouth worked, curving slowly into a hastly smile. "Guess. Again."

Kayla's voice caught in her throat, but she forced erself to say it. "Golias?"

"Now you understand."

Briefly she probed within herself, searching for ome trace, some hint of the mindghost's presence.

She could find nothing, nothing at all. He was one. But hadn't he fooled her once before? Yes, Gol-as had let her think that he had left her when in fact e had been quiescent, awaiting a rekindling. "No," she said. "Gods, no. You can't do this, Golias. It's a bad joke."

"No joke. Only way to save Salome, others."

The arms were twitching spasmodically, fingers writhing like worms, a terrible sight.

"Can't you at least try to get that body under better control?"

"Am trying."

He flailed around in a backward spin, nearly falling out of the bed.

"Be careful, Golias."

"D–difficult."

Kayla watched the body jerk and shudder, and knew she needed help.

"Just stay right here. Stop moving. Do you hear me, Golias? Don't move."

She raced out to the com kiosk and punched in Lyle MacKenzie's number.

Iger answered on the first ring.

"Iger, thank the gods . . ."

He hung up.

Cursing, she redialed. Somebody—Iger?—answered.

Before he could speak she said, "Iger, please listen to me! Forgive me, Iger. I was wrong. You're right, you're right, I was crazy. I just couldn't handle the thought that I had killed our only chance of finding the others."

His expression was wary, but there was a grudging ɔok of acceptance in the blue eyes. "And now?"

"Now you've got to get down here to the hospital ight away. I need you."

"What's happened?"

"I'll explain when you get here."

"What about Mac?"

"Call Darius Peters and get some of his men to tay there. But get down here!"

"I'm on my way."

* * *

Kayla and Iger sat together in the pale green hospi- al room and watched "Keller" stagger across the loor.

"I thought you told me that he was brain dead," ger said. "He moves around pretty well for some- ody suffering from complete synapse lapse."

Kayla took a deep breath. "Iger, believe me, that's ot Yates Keller."

"No?" He smirked at her. "Then tell me, who is ? Pelleas Karlson?"

"I mean it, Iger. Yates Keller *is* brain dead. That's e mindghost, Golias, in his body."

"What?"

"Shh. Not so loud, you'll get the medics in here. lobody else knows."

"Dammit, Katie, are you sure?"

"Pretty sure."

"That's not sure enough."

"I can't get back in to probe. Golias has erected some kind of shield. That in itself is an indication it's him. Keller never could have shielded himself from me. His mindpowers were too weak. That's why he wanted me."

"I didn't think a mindghost had empathic powers."

"Maybe they're vestigial powers that he retains from the Mindstar. Maybe he picked them up from me. Who knows?"

Iger shook his head. "If I hadn't seen him move your body around when your mind got trapped elsewhere, I wouldn't listen to you for a minute. But I believe you, Katie. Gods help us all." He frowned as Keller/Golias stumbled past him. "Hey, Golias, you're going to have to do a better job than that if you expect to get out of here."

Kayla grabbed the dybbuck's arm. "Golias, stop it. Just stop moving for a minute and answer some questions."

The body sat down heavily upon the foot of the bed.

"Can you reach any of Keller's memories?" she asked.

The voice was thick, as though the tongue moved only with difficulty. "Don't know. Trying. Flashes See flashes, like holo show. Pieces."

"That's not good enough."

The body held up a wobbling hand. "Wait. Time."

"We don't have time!"

Clumsily, but with more control than before, "Kel-r" stood. Mouth set in concentration, he walked to e door, turned with just a slight hesitation, and alked back. The hands were still trembling slightly. Better?" he said.

"Yes," Kayla said. "But we need the memories, olias. Concentrate on the memories!"

"Trying. I'm. Trying."

"What do you see? What's in there?"

"I see flashes. Dark. A cave. Two people. Your par-nts. The rocks begin falling."

"No! I don't want to hear about that!" Kayla ulled away, covering her ears. "Stop it! Stop it, Gol-s." Tears flooded her eyes and threatened to spill own her face.

Iger put his arms around her. "Katie, we have to o this. For Salome, and the others. Come on." He ook her gently and turned back to the dybbuk.

"Golias," he said. "Look for a woman with dark kin and golden hair. A beautiful woman, Golias, ith eyes like big amber gems. Salome. You remem-er her. And a man as tall as a giant Orkima plant. g, dark hair, beard. Barabbas. Salome and Rab. And ok for the red-haired musician, Arsobades. The ree of them."

"Looking." The dybbuk's eyes were squeezed

tightly in concentration. "Salome. Barabbas Arsobades."

Kayla leaned close. "Yes? Golias, what do you see?"

"See them."

"Where?" It came out in a shout. Kayla had to restrain herself from grabbing at him in her eagerness. "Where are they?"

"Dark. Wet."

"Wet? What do you mean?"

"Can't tell. Wet."

"Where is it?"

"Far."

"You'll have to do better than that."

"Far. Can't say."

"How far?"

"Bandar. Bandar Sabya." He opened his eyes and stared at Kayla. "Bandar Sabya."

"But there's on the other side of St. Ilban," Iger said. "Nobody goes there. Nobody lives there."

Kayla stared intently at the dybbuk. "Where in Bandar Sabya? Where, Golias?"

"Can't see." He wavered. "Too hard. Too far."

And before he could say more, his eyes closed and he toppled backward onto the bed.

Iger stared at Kayla, and she stared back.

"Now what?" he said. "Call the medics? Wait and see if he revives?"

"Let's sit him up." Kayla grabbed an arm, bu

"Keller" sagged like a sack of bambera feed. "Oof, he's a dead weight. Help me, Iger."

Iger reached out to support the inert body. "See what you mean. He's heavy all right."

Together they manhandled the body to a sitting position on the bed-cum-gurney.

"Golias, can you hear me?" Kayla shouted. "C'mon, get back here."

The body moaned.

"Golias!"

She tried a mindprobe, but it bounced back at her, shards of mental energy, all reflecting her own face, her own mind signature, stabbing at her like pieces of broken glass.

"Dammit," she said. "This is no good. We've got to get him out of here."

Iger stared at her. "Out of the hospital? What do you suggest, kidnapping him?"

"Exactly."

"We won't get ten feet. Everybody recognizes that face. They all know Yates Keller."

"Maybe they won't see it."

"I thought you told me that you can't manage that sense-fogging shadowfield stuff anymore."

"I won't have to." She smiled. "Now comb your hair and go flirt with the head nurse."

"What?"

She took him by the shoulders and propelled him into the washroom. "I need a diversion, Iger. You can provide it. Just radiate that old Liagean charm." As further motivation she pinched him, hard, on the cheek.

He fiddled with his ponytail, retied the thong holding it, and brushed off his tunic. "What should I say?"

"I don't care. Propose to her. Marry her, if you have to. Just keep her away from here for the next fifteen minutes." She surveyed him and nodded. "Fine. Now remember, meet me back here in fifteen minutes."

Iger sighed. "I don't believe this."

"Think sex. You know how to do that." Kayla waggled her fingers at him. "Now get out there and break hearts."

As he walked out the door, she began to ransack the room, pulling out drawers, pawing through cabinets.

There. A tube of bandage plasm.

She triggered it, released a great fizzing mass of creamy liquid bandage, and set to work.

* * *

Iger came back in exactly fifteen minutes. "Kayla ... what the hell?" His eyes widened in surprise.

Yates Keller lay upon a gurney, his features completely obscured by a masklike mass of bandages.

Kayla stood next to him, grinning. She wore a medic's blue stretchsuit.

"Here." She tossed a similar suit at Iger. "Put this on. And don't forget the air mask."

"Where did you find these?"

"A laundry mech, making a delivery. They won't miss these." She pulled the mask up over the bottom of her face, and settled the blue hood of her suit over her hair. "Good." Her voice was slightly muffled, but that wouldn't matter. "You ready?"

Iger's hair was tucked away into his hood, and his mask covered him up to his eyes. "Yeah."

"Try to look down, don't look anybody in the eye. We've got to get Keller out of here and to the spaceport."

"Spaceport?"

"Shhh. Not so loud. Let's go. And remember, it's a medical emergency. Severe quarantine situation. Just say that if anybody tries to stop us."

They activated the bed's mechgurney function and, walking along on either side of it, accompanied "Keller" out into the hall. The nurses didn't so much as look up as they passed.

Casually, Kayla buzzed for the elevator.

"So far, so good," Iger muttered.

"Shh!"

The lift arrived, and they hustled their burden into the narrow compartment. As the doors of the lift closed, voices could be heard in the hall beyond, voices raised in concern.

"Hit the express button," Kayla said. "And be prepared to move when we reach the basement."

"The basement?"

"Would you rather waltz out the main entrance where a thousand people can see us, and risk getting caught? No thanks."

"Where are we taking him?"

"The *Antimony*."

"What?"

"I don't want medics sniffing around, subjecting him to tests. If he regains consciousness, I want him to be where I can ask questions."

The hiss of brakes reverberated through the small compartment. A moment later the doors slid open, and Kayla and Iger gazed out into a maze of winding, poorly lit hallways.

"Hope you know the way out," Iger said.

"We'll find it, we'll find it." Kayla hit the override button on the gurney and took control, quickly guiding it out of the elevator.

The basement was a silent warren of forgotten holo files stacked cube upon cube. A final stop where deactivated mechs leaned one against the other like sad, drunken, earless mice, and dead screens, some cracked, others missing their frames, stood propped in rows awaiting some vanished repairman. A thin layer of velvety dust coated everything. The dry, musty air had a faint vinegar tang of old disinfectant.

Iger sniffed and sneezed. "So this is where they keep the past. Doesn't look like they visit it much either."

"Would you?"

His blue eyes danced above the mask. "Certain select portions, definitely."

Kayla shook her head. "The past is a trap and nostalgia is a luxury I don't have any time for."

Iger said nothing in response but sneezed twice.

On the gurney, the dybbuk "Keller" groaned softly.

In silence they wheeled him through the dusty gloom. A faint brightening ahead promised fresh air, an exit. They hurried toward it.

"What are you doing down here with that patient?"

The voice was abrupt, authoritative, and the speaker matched the voice. A trim woman with brown hair and sharp features barred their way. "Well? I asked you a question."

"Medical emergency," Iger said.

"Emergency? No patients come down here. Everybody knows that. Show me your ID badges."

"Who are you?" Kayla said.

"I'm the chief administrator for the central wing." She held out her hand. "Badges, please."

Kayla took a deep breath and mindbolted her.

The woman's eyes rolled back and up until only the whites were showing. She slid to the floor, unconscious. Kayla tipped her up against the wall and slid the gurney past.

"Lucky shot," Iger said.

"Let's hope I don't have to do it again. That took almost everything I had."

The exit was ahead. Nearly running, they burst through it and across a side street where only a lone ambulance idled, its attendant unconcerned with two passing medics and their unconscious patient.

Kayla and Iger sidled past, moved down the street, and crossed into a mech ambulance yard.

"Perfect," she said. "Just what we need."

They moved through the yard, trying doors.

"Here!" Iger called.

An unlocked ambulance. They hoisted "Keller" into the back of it and climbed aboard.

"Where to?" the mech navboard inquired.

"Vardalia Port, berth 71–A."

The fusion engine came on, purring.

Iger pulled the doors shut.

They rode in considerable comfort, the mech navboard moving the vehicle smoothly through the streets, its sensors enabling it to avoid potholes, gunfights, and other obstacles.

However, one thing that it was not able to avoid was the security checkpoint at Vardalia Port.

Kayla and Iger sat motionless in the ambulance.

Their false ID wouldn't get them past the port entrance and they knew it.

"ID, please." It was the same officious clerk as before. He stared into the ambulance cab without any obvious signs of recognition.

Kayla took a deep breath and prepared to release another mindbolt.

"Vardalia Central Hospital," the ambulance said. "Registry VCH2451."

The clerk waved them past without another glance.

"I love this van," Iger said. "I want to marry it."

"Shhh."

The ferry up-station was waiting, ready lights blinking red-gold, red-gold.

Kayla and Iger unloaded the ambulance quickly.

"Iger, take Keller onto the ferry," Kayla said. "I'll be right behind you."

She leaned back into the ambulance cab, told the mech driver to erase its travel log and return to the hospital. It beeped twice and sped away.

Kayla felt a ridiculous impulse to wave. Turning, she hopped aboard the ferry and settled in for the brief trip to the ship berths.

"Berths 63–A to 83–A," announced the mech conductor.

"That's our stop," Iger said.

Kayla nudged the gurney and with Iger beside her, followed it onto the docks.

71–A.

Kayla stared at the gleaming bulk of the *Antimony.* It would never replace the *Falstaff* in her affection, but she had rarely been as happy to see a ship.

"I don't believe we made it," Iger said.

"Me either. C'mon, let's get our patient safely aboard."

Chapter Seventeen

The *Antimony* was a peaceful world under complete mech control. In ops, gleaming relays and blinking boards ran smoothly under the knowbot's guidance. Kayla gave it all an appreciative glance and took a deep breath of metallic shipboard air.

Third Child came ambling into ops, chirping happily.

"Glad to see you, too," Kayla said. "How do you feel?"

"Quirch!"

Kayla turned to Iger for translation.

"I think that means okay."

"No more nausea or hallucinations? Good."

On the gurney, "Keller" moaned and said something.

"What's that?" Kayla asked. "What's he mumbling?"

"Can't get it." Iger leaned closer. "It's about Rab and Salome."

"Tired," "Keller" said. "Can't hold out."

"Does he mean them or him? Gods, this is maddening!"

Third Child chirped again and came closer, peering excitedly at the dybbuk.

"Keller's" eyelids twitched and opened. He sat up, quivering, blinked rapidly, and exhaled hard.

"Where. Am. I?"

"The *Antimony,*" Kayla said.

His eyes roved from face to face, back and forth, coming to rest upon the dalkoi.

"Close."

"What? What's close?"

The dybbuk gestured at Third Child, hands opening and closing as though he would grasp the dalkoi. His meaning was unmistablable. "Closer. Come closer."

The dalkoi blinked. Its chirp was a frightened whisper. It pulled back swiftly and began to move toward the door.

"Closer!" There was anguish in "Keller's" voice now. "Please. I need you."

Kayla reached out and caught Third Child by her vestigial shoulder. "Don't worry. There's nothing to fear. We're right here with you. Just lean toward him."

Third Child's purple eyes scanned hers as though searching for truth.

"Really," Iger echoed. "It's safe. We're here."

Slowly the dalkoi inclined its triangular head nearer to the reclining figure of the dybbuk. "Quirch!"

"Yes." "Keller" nodded rapidly. "Yes, this is better. I can hear them. I can hear them, now. Underground. They're in a large room. No doors. No windows."

"In Bandar Sabya?" Kayla said.

"Yes."

"Iger, plot a course."

"We're taking the *Antimony*?"

"Yeah, we'll hover, using the mini-shuttle to land. It's the fastest way."

"Immediate liftoff? Vardalia Port's gonna love this."

"Screw 'em."

"What if they don't give us flight-path clearance?"

"Then we go without their permission. Blast out of here if we have to."

"Okay." His lips were a thin, compressed line.

Kayla knew what Iger thought—that he disapproved—but she didn't care. They were going to find Salome and the others if she had to leave Vardalia Port in smoking ruins.

"Course laid in," he said.

"Notify Port Authority that we're leaving."

"Priority message coming in."

"Ignore it." She was intent on the systems board, monitoring the ship's readying process.

"Katie," Iger said. "It's about Mac."

"What?" She looked up, startled. "What's happened?"

"Somebody's tried to shoot him again. Darius Peters requests our presence immediately."

"Dammit. Try and raise him."

"He's not answering."

Kayla bit her lip. She could waste more time—perhaps vital time—attempting to protect Lyle MacKenzie. Or she could leave that problem in the hands of Darius Peters and abandon MacKenzie, going instead to Bandar Sabya, as planned.

I'm sorry, Mac, she thought. *Finding Salome and the others has priority.*

Aloud, she said, "Power up for liftoff."

Iger's glance was more than a trifle accusatory. "We're just going to leave? Desert Mac?"

"We'll be back." She stared implacably at her screen. "And the faster we get going, the faster we'll get back."

The *Antimony*'s engines went to full power, purring gently. "Five seconds to liftoff," Iger said. "Four. Three. Two. One. Ignition."

Kayla felt the gentle push of gravity shove her backward in her webseat as the ship cleared Vardalia Port and rose above the city. As they swung into the turn to bring them south and west, aimed for Bandar Sabya, she began to smile.

We're coming, friends, she thought. *Just hold on a ittle bit longer.*

* * *

Bandar Sabya was a crescent-shaped island conti-
nent in the southern White Sea, isolated both geo-
graphically and politically. The few residents who
ived there were fiercely private, refusing all but the
nost necessary contact with Vardalia.

As the *Antimony* hovered, Kalyla stared at the
creen, scanning for possible landing sites for the
nini-shuttle. She saw the rust-colored geometric pat-
erns of habitats but nothing that provided the rein-
orced landing pad that the shuttle required. She
vould have to improvise.

"Golias," she said. "Can you get any fix on
ocation?"

The dybbuk also stared at the screen with intense
oncentration, its furrowed brow giving it an inad-
ertent look of agony. "Ask Third Child to stand
loser to me." He was speaking in full sentences
now. His mastery of the body was improving mo-
nent by moment.

"Third Child," Kayla called. "Get over here."

The dalkoi hung back for a moment, still obviously
ıneasy about the dybbuk. But as Kayla gestured im-
atiently, Third Child padded over until she stood
eside "Keller."

"Better," he said. "Hmmm. No direct fix on location, yet. But I have a stronger sense of where they probably are. That settlement, there." He indicated a mottled huddling of low buildings. "That's the place."

"Iger, you heard him. That's where I'll go in."

"*We'll* go in. You're not doing this alone."

"But—"

"No arguments, Katie." His eyes were blue ice. "Or I'll take us back to Vardalia Port, pronto."

She glared at him, but he only shrugged.

"Okay," she said. "If you insist. Park this bucket in hover mode. We're all going planetside."

"Even Third Child?"

"You saw how she helps Golias access Keller's memory. We need her."

"If you say so." He locked the navboard into sync with the knowbot in control once more. "Weapons?"

"As many as you can carry."

"Magnum disruptors, too?"

"The works. We may have to shoot our way in—and out."

Iger nodded. "Okay."

"I'll take care of Golias," she said. "You handle Third Child, okay?"

"Right." He strapped on a laser pistol, and tied another to his right leg just above the knee.

Kayla strapped on a pistol and two disruptors.

Now," she said. "Let's go get Salome, Rab, and
.rsobades."

The mini-shuttle was heavily laden, which might
ave accounted for its sluggish response to controls.
ger was forced to handle the navboard manually.

Onscreen, the rusted crescent of Bandar Sabya
pread, colors and structures becoming steadily more
istinct as the shuttle flew lower through the
tmosphere.

The shuttle cut below the mottled cloud cover to
woop over the rust-gray landscape. Its landing jets
attened the spindly bushes and odd, spidery trees
ative only to Bandar Sabya.

Kayla had selected a sun-baked salt flat as the most
romising landing site. It swelled from a distant
andy curve until it filled the screen.

"Landing in ten seconds," Iger said. "Nine.
ight . . ."

Whump!

Kayla swung wildly in her webset. The lights
ickered and went out. Somewhere there was the
mell of burning connectors. The dalkoi was twit-
ering loudly behind her and "Keller" thrashed in
is webcouch. "Shit!" Iger said.

The hiss of the fire mechs filled the darkness. Mo-
nents later, emergency globes flooded the shuttle in-
erior with sickly yellow-green light as the "all-clear"
ignal sounded.

"What the hell happened?" Kayla demanded.

Iger looked at her, his face flushed. "We came in faster than I thought."

"And landed harder." She unbuckled herself and began a systems check. "I hope we'll be able to take off again."

Iger nodded, busy at the navboard. "Systems look okay," he said, his voice hoarse with relief. "A few are on backup, but most are okay. We'll be able to achieve escape velocity and reach the *Antimony* easy."

"Good." Kayla popped the hatch. "Everybody out."

Dry, hot air blew in.

It was an odd group that straggled through the open mouth of the shuttle and onto the long sand spit: a young man with long blond hair spilling down his back and a young woman with a short brush of red hair, both bristling with armament, followed by a two-legged lavender dalkoi hopping from foot to foot, and a shambling brain-dead body inhabited by a mindghost. Golias/Keller could walk, after a fashion, dragging one leg along, stomping upon the good foot, nearly falling, only to catch himself again and again. It wasn't graceful, but it was locomotion.

They walked in silence, sand grains crunching underfoot, the hot wind pushing against them. Then Kayla cried out. "You there! Stop!"

A man in pale robes turned to glare at them. He made as if to turn away, and Kayla called out again

"Wait! We're strangers here. We need your help."

Now the man did turn. And ran. He raced away from them as fast as the sand permitted. Before Kayla could draw a disruptor to try to stop him, he had disappeared behind a grayish dune.

"Damn!"

Iger hurried after the vanished stranger, but he was gone.

"We won't let the next one get away as easily," Kayla said. "Golias, are you reading anything?"

"Sorry, Kate. Nothing yet."

"Dammit, we need to talk to somebody who lives here."

A head appeared around the curve of a dune. Ducked back into hiding. Emerged slowly.

Kayla cried out, "You! Don't run. Please! We're peaceful. We just want to find some friends here."

"Friends?" The head emerged, followed by the body. He was dressed in several layers of gray robes, his face baked dark by the twin suns, his hair bleached to golden whiteness.

"Friends, yes. Have you seen any strangers come here?"

He took a step closer. "Strangers, like you?"

"Yes. Well, no. A beautiful woman, dark-skinned, golden-haired. A tall man—a giant, really. Bearded. Fierce-looking. And a shorter man, with bright red hair and a beard. A singer and musician."

The native shrugged noncommittally. "Maybe I did and maybe I didn't."

"Please. It's very important." She watched his eyes flickering over them, sizing them up. "We can pay you."

"Vardalian money?" The native spit. "Ain't worth nothing here. What else you got?" He eyed their weapons with greedy and obvious interest.

Kayla let him look. Then, casually pocketing her laser pistol, she said, "You show me where my friends are, and maybe then we'll talk about trading some guns."

The native nodded eagerly. "Strangers, yes. Come." He beckoned, his attention upon them but his body leaning away toward a distant row of buildings.

"In there?" Kayla asked.

"Keller" muttered beside her, "No. Something's not right. Not there."

"Here, yes, here," the native said.

"Kate," "Keller" said. "I'm getting some sense of their location but it's not in those buildings."

Iger leaned toward them. "Is he lying to us? Setting us up to be jumped?"

Kayla formed a tiny mindprobe and nimbly pierced the stranger's consciousness.

He had no idea where Salome and the others were. His thoughts were full of weapons, of trapping and killing her little party, and taking their armaments.

Bastard, she thought.

Before they took another step she grabbed his mind in a steely, punishing grip.

He gasped once and sank to the sand, unconscious.

"So much for our guide," Iger said. "You did that?"

"He was going to kill us."

"Keller" staggered, moaning. "Dark," he said. "Dark and cold. Weak."

Silently, Kayla guided Third Child toward the dybbuk.

"Keller" straightened up. "They're in that town. That way." He pointed toward a distant row of buildings nearly invisible in the sea mist.

"That way?" Kayla said. "Let's move it."

They hurried into the deserted settlement, following the dybbuk's muttered instructions.

"Left," said the dybbuk. "Right here. Down this alley. Across and over there. It's coming from there."

"There" was a battered building, stained and pockmarked. A faded title carved in old-style script upon the pediment above the door said: Bandar Sabya Desalinization Works.

Chapter Eighteen

The door was locked and barred.

Kayla unstrapped her magnum disruptor. "Stand back," she told the others. "I'm going to blow it down."

One blast from the disruptor shattered the frame. The next blew the entire door right out of its casing.

The entrance yawned open into darkness like a cave mouth, giving off cold air. But Third Child hung back at the entrance and "Keller" made no move to enter.

"Come on," Kayla said. "This is what we came for." She stepped inside, sniffed, and wrinkled her nose. The chill air smelled of wet mold and unwashed bodies confined for too long. Beside her, Iger sneezed.

"What is this place?" he asked.

"Nothing good," Kayla snapped. "Let's move."

Flicking on the glowlamp attached to her disruptor, she strode boldly into the dark building.

The only sound was that of water dripping. Grit rasped underfoot.

The building brought back a jumble of bad memories for Kayla. It reeked of food gone rancid, backed-up plumbing, and hopelessly confined lives.

Obviously, it had lately been used as a prison. Why had the Bandar Sabyans allowed it? Had Yates Keller paid them off? And where were the local citizens? In hiding? Dead?

She and Iger moved quickly through the darkened hallways until they came to a locked door. Another disruptor blast and the door was a memory.

Kayla moved through into the chill dark.

The floor gave way beneath her. At least, that was how it felt to her.

She could hear Iger calling her, faintly, from a great distance and she wanted to reply, wanted desperately to call to him. But she was caught in a web of interlocking fragmented images that prevented her from speaking or even moving.

A monstrous eye blinked and, behind it, receding back into swirls, a hundred eyes blinked.

A hand dashed away a tear and a thousand hands wiped a thousand sorrows.

Whose tears? Whose eyes?

Mine, Kayla thought. *All mine.*

A thousand sorrows I've never cried for, never had the time, never wanted to claim.

All the hard and ugly things she'd done, never

questioning, never stopping even to think. Feeling had been a luxury.

But now she had all the time she had lacked.

She could repent her crimes at length.

* * *

"I don't understand it," Iger said. "She just disappeared. It's like she went through an invisible door somewhere."

Third Child chirped loudly in alarm. Beside her, the dybbuk "Keller" was thrashing in agitation.

"Well of sorrow," "Keller" managed. "Mindtrap. Set for Katie. Yates Keller thought she'd come here."

"A mindtrap? Why not a conventional one?"

"Keller" shrugged. "Reasons gone now."

"How do I get her out?"

Again the dybbuk shrugged.

"I'm going in after her."

"Could be dangerous."

"No choice, is there?" Iger didn't wait for a reply. He plunged into the darkness and found himself—standing in darkness. The mindtrap didn't ensnare him. A moment later he retreated, sheepishly, back to Third Child and the dybbuk.

"It doesn't want me."

"Then it's set for Katie. Katie, only."

"What's this thing made of?"

"Mindstones."

"Mindstones?" Iger paused. He recalled a scene: a park in Vardalia, a circle of well-to-do citizens watching a musical performance. A crowd studded in mindstones. And then, one by one, the mindstones began to lose their luster, turn ashen and gray, wink and go dead.

"Third Child!" he cried. "Third Child, get your purple butt over here!"

The dalkoi whimpered and backpedaled.

"Not so fast." Iger grasped her by the throat. "This job was made for you."

"Quirch!"

"There's nothing to be afraid of! You saw that the trap didn't hurt me. And it won't hurt you either. It doesn't want you. It just wants Katie."

Third Child made a sound that might have been stoic resignation, or a belch.

"Come on." Iger towed the dalkoi back with him into the darkness.

* * *

Like an uneasy sleepwalker, Kayla made her way among the refracted images of her past.

Her parents, dressed for a day in the mines. Greer, her former roomate, racing across the Grand Plaza of Vardalia. Rusty Turlay, the mute medium of the Vardalian groupmind. Little Shotay, former owner of the Mindstar, and Mogul, the prison guard who killed her. Silver-haired Evlin, the dancer who lost his mind because of the Mindstar. Pelleas Karlson, who lost his soul. Yates Keller.

The dead and those-as-good-as-dead. Hers.

All of them, hers.

Ghostly images flitted past, images of Salome, Rab, and Arsobades.

No. No, she wouldn't accept that. They were still alive, they had to be.

But weren't they her victims as well?

Kayla's long-damned emotions crested and overflowed. She was flooded with aching regret, with gut-stabbing longing, with guilt, with sorrow, with pain.

So many things she could have done differently. Would have.

—I could have been kinder.

—More responsive and aware.

—Protected them.

And the tormenting echoes danced in her head: protected, protected, protected them.

Alone in the dark with only her sins for company, Kayla sank to her knees and wept.

* * *

With one hand, Iger lofted the glowglobe and stared at the strange circular framework suspended from the ceiling. Matte black, it was studded by mindstones that gave it the appearance of an enormous jeweled crown.

Within the circle was an opaque field of intense darkness whose center concealed Katie. But Iger could neither pass into it nor shut down the field.

He used his other hand to shove the protesting Third Child toward the nearest stones. "There," he said. "Go on. Have a big time."

Third Child stared reproachfully at the stone. Then its neck, already long, seemed to elongate further. Gently, the dalkoi rubbed its nose against the ruby-blue-bronze gem.

Almost immediately, the stone's lights faded. In moments it had gone gray and dead.

"Quirch!"

"That's it," Iger said. "Keep going."

Third Child hurried to the next stone. In a moment she had absorbed its dazzle as well. And so the dalkoi went around the circle, stone by stone, extinguishing each one with a chirp of delight, growing more animated by the moment.

Around the circle, the mindstones turned to mere ashen ghosts of their former brilliance. And Third Child glowed with ever increasing vigor, her skin giving off a faint lavender aura, her purple eyes sparkling.

The darkness at the heart of the circle was beginning to wane, thinning to a grayish fog, dissipating. Within the circle, at its center, a figure was kneeling.

"I can see her!" Iger cried.

Without waiting for the dalkoi to finish her task, he plunged into the mist, seized Kayla's arm, and hauled her to her feet. When she made no effort to move further, he pulled her free of the mindtrap.

"Don't stop, Third Child!" he said. "Get every stone."

"Quirch!"

"I don't care if you're not hungry anymore."

He didn't stay to see if the dalkoi complied but dragged Kayla out into the corridor.

"Katie?" He shook her until she turned her face up to his and he saw that there were tears on her cheeks. "What did that bastard do to you?"

Her voice was thick as she answered, "It's over now." And, to Iger's vast amazement, she put her arms around his neck and buried her face against his chest, weeping as though her heart had been broken. He patted her awkwardly.

"Hey, it's okay. I'm here. Shhh."

The storm subsided as quickly as it had come on. Sniffing, Kayla pulled out of his arms.

"Better?"

She nodded and dried her eyes. "Let's go."

* * *

The building went deeper into the ground and the corridors wound in upon themselves, leading to blind walls from which it was necessary to double back.

Kayla and Iger searched in the dark, calling to their friends, receiving no reply.

"Try a mindprobe?"

"I can't," Kayla said. "Remember Salome's sensitivity? She'll start convulsing. We can't risk that."

"Yeah. Guess we keep searching the old-fashioned way. Gods, this is frustrating."

And behind them came Third Child, sniffing at every door frame, and "Keller," shambling yet looking more and more human—until you peered into his eyes.

It was Third Child who stopped at a locked door, whinnying.

"There's nothing there," Iger said. "Come on."

The dalkoi refused to budge.

"We already checked it."

"Quirch!"

"All right. I'll show you." Iger pulled his disruptor from its holster and took aim.

ZZZAT!

The big gun blew the door away and took some of the door frame with it.

"Gods!" Iger said. He stepped inside.

Kayla was right behind him.

Something was huddled in a far corner.

Slowly it resolved into three distinct shapes, three shadows humped together in misery.

"Salome!" Kayla cried. "Rab! Arsobades!"

Oh, gods, gods, gods, it *was* them.

With tentative, shuffling steps her former shipmates came tottering forward. But they had been transformed.

Salome's dark beauty had dimmed. Her skin was ashen, her golden hair matted. She gazed at Kayla with dull eyes but somehow managed a weak smile.

"At last," she whispered.

Rab loomed closer, still tall, big-boned, but the flesh hung upon him like a loose stretchsuit. His beard reached to his chest and his hair was a dark, wild tangle. "Katie, is it you? Really you? I don't believe it." He peered into her face as if he refused to give credence to what he saw. "We thought we'd really had it this time. Keller's goons abandoned us here weeks ago. I won't tell you how we've survived this long."

Even Arsobades, the rotund minstrel, was down to skin and bones, the planes of his face standing out in sharp relief behind his beard. "If I ever eat another bug, so help me, I *will* die. I'll kill my goddamned self."

"We'll get you back to the *Antimony*," Kayla said. Her voice felt untrustworthy and tears filled her eyes. "No more buts, I promise."

But Salome had turned accusing eyes upon her. "Another week and we'd have been done for. I'm not sure that I trust this so-called rescue."

"What do you mean?"

"I mean, Katie, where were you? Why should I trust you now when you were probably the one who set us up in the first place? What did it get you? The *Falstaff*?"

"Salome!" Kayla recoiled, wounded. But her former captain was relentless.

"You set us up," Salome insisted. "Set us up and abandoned us. Now you show, now, when we're nearly finished. To give us false hope before the next round." Tears began to leak from the corners of her eyes. "But we've got nothing to tell anybody. We would have told it all long ago."

Rab pulled her close and the once-proud pirate hid her face in the folds of his rags.

"Salome," Kayla cried. "You've got to believe me. I had nothing to do with this. Nothing! I've been searching for you this entire time."

The looks that Rab and Arsobades gave her were deeply suspicious.

"Be reasonable. Why would I sell you out to Keller and his men?"

"That's what we'd all like to know," Rab said.

"You're wrong."

"Yeah?" Arsobades cocked his head at the dybbuk "Keller." "Then what's that son-of-a-bitch doing here?"

Rab pulled Salome behind him. "What is this, Katie? Another trap?"

"No trap, Rab." She out her hands, pleading. "All of you, please, listen to me. It's not what you think. That's not Yates Keller."

"What are you saying?" Rab demanded. "He's standing right here in front of us."

"That's just his body."

"His body?" Rab seemed stunned.

Salome peered around the bulk of her lover. "Have you lost your mind, Katie?"

"No. But you could say that Keller has." Quickly Kayla explained about mindbolting Yates Keller, about Golias, and the dybbuk standing before them.

"I know it's hard to believe," she said. "But do you think I would have him here with me otherwise? Keller's gone. He's an empty shell. That's the mind-ghost, Golias, in there. He's been able to gain access to Keller's memories. It's the only way I could ever have found you."

Rab gave a wary nod. "Okay. That's such a wild story that I'll believe it, for the time being. But the minute he starts to act like Keller, I'll bash his frigging head in."

"Just keep him away from me," Arsobades said. "I don't like seeing that bastard's face, regardless of who's in there doing the driving. And I'm still not sure that I believe you, Kate. I don't believe anybody, anymore."

"Will you at least let me rescue you?"

Wearily, he nodded.

Kayla herded the group out of the building and along the dusty street. Weakened by their incarceration, the *Falstaff*'s crew couldn't move very quickly.

"We've just got to get to the beach," Kayla said. "Just a little bit farther. The shuttle is waiting."

They moved along the street in silence.

"Freeze, all of you."

The voice was shocking in the quiet air, yet oddly familiar. But Kayla couldn't quite place it.

A tall blonde woman dressed in dusty coveralls stepped out of the shelter of a rickety lean-to. She held a magnum disruptor with both hands, trained upon them.

Just one woman? Kayla thought. *She must be kidding. I'll drop her in her tracks.*

As she reached for her gun, a second voice came from behind her: "Don't."

A short man in an iridescent stretchsuit held a laser pistol that looked almost too large for his hand.

Rab made an angry sound deep in his throat.

Kayla flicked a hand at him: *No berserker rages, Rab, not here.* "Who are you?" she said to the strangers. "Who are you and what do you want?"

"We want to talk to Keller. We know he came here with you. We followed your ship."

Kayla strangled the hysterical laughter that was building in her throat. "Keller? You want to talk to *him*?"

"Yes. Why is that so peculiar? We have a proposal that we think will interest him."

"What if he doesn't want to talk to you?"

"We'll let him decide."

Disgusted, Kayla said, "Oh, all right."

Iger flashed Kayla a warning look but she shook her head slightly. "Keller, these people want to talk to *you.*"

The dybbuk turned to face them.

"Raintree and Fichu," said the woman. "We've worked together before."

Briefly a light came to "Keller's" eyes. His mouth worked for a moment. "R–raintree? Coral Raintree? And Robard Fichu? Yes, yes, I remember you. You were Karlson's agents. Secret police. What do you want?"

The two stared, obviously surprised by the condition of their quarry.

"What happened to you?" Raintree asked.

Kayla stepped forward. "Slight vascular cerebral accident. Nothing to be concerned about. Just affects his speech. And his movements. But the mind is as sharp as ever."

The smaller man—Fichu?—gave her a sour, suspicious glance.

She shrugged.

"Keller, we want to talk to you privately."

"Keller" shook his head. "Here."

Raintree sighed loudly. "All right." She lowered

her gun. "We want to strike a deal about the mindsalt. All the mines on Styx have been closed. The bars in Vardalia—those selling mindsalt—have been shut down. The supply is dwindling. There's never been such a perfect market."

"Why come to me?" The dybbuk's voice was only slightly slurred. His control over the body was improving steadily.

"You're the only one who can circumvent Merrick the Blackbird," Raintree said. "You've always had access to the mines."

Kayla cut in. "Why not just strike a deal with Merrick? I'll bet he'd like to get those mines working again."

"He's not interested in deals," said Fichu. "He wants control of everything. And all of the profits."

"Now is the moment to do it," Raintree repeated. "We can seize it all, the entire market. Cut off Merrick. Deal directly with our own people. By the time the bars reopen, we'll be the only game in town."

To Kayla's amazement, the dybbuk "Keller" was nodding and smiling.

"It's a good plan," he said. "I'd like to hear more."

"What?" she cried. Was the dybbuk trying to buy them time or had he turned traitor?

Raintree raised her weapon again. "You heard him."

Fichu fidgeted with his pistol. "What should we do with the rest of them?"

"No survivors," Raintree said. "All lost at sea."

Fichu raised his pistol, took aim.

Third Child chirped, hiccuped twice, and keeled over.

Fichu's weapon jerked aside.

Iger drew his laser pistol and shot the gun out of Fichu's hands. Fichu gasped.

Iger reached for him, but he ducked and began running toward Coral Raintree. Arsobades stuck out his leg and tripped the little man as he scrambled past him. The two of them went down, sprawling, in the red dust.

Kayla jumped Raintree, bringing her down with a slashing kick that knocked the disruptor out of her hand.

The dybbuk "Keller" began to wave his arms and shake wildly. Rab grabbed hold of him, hugging his former enemy in an attempt to restrain his wilder gyrations.

The dalkoi lay motionless in the red dust.

"Third Child!" Iger cried. He shook the dalkoi gently. "Answer me!"

There was no response.

Kayla said, "We'll have to carry her."

"What about these two?" Arsobades asked, indicating Fichu and Raintree.

"Let's leave them here for the natives to deal with." Kayla secured Raintree's hands behind her back. "Disable their shuttle. I'm sure the natives can scavenge it for spare parts."

"You'll be guilty of murder," Fichu said, wincing as Arsobades tied him to a stanchion.

"Not if you're really good negotiators," Kayla said. She nodded to her companions. "Let's go."

Raintree and Fichu's protests died behind them.

In minutes they were on the beach. The *Antimony*'s shuttle sat quietly on the gray sand, waiting.

Salome squinted at the craft. "Can that little thing hold all of us?"

Arsobades shook his head. "No way."

"Iger, make two trips," Kayla said quickly. "I'll wait here with Golias." She ignored Rab's suspicious glance. "Get everybody safely up to the ship and come back for me."

* * *

The twin suns hung low over the ocean, igniting the waters with a brief dazzling show of orange brilliance before sinking below the horizon line. Only the purple curve of ever-present Xenobe remained in the sky, paled to lavender by ocean mist.

Deep shadows crept across the land, turning the dust and vegetation pearly gray. The stars began to peep through the clouds. Anxiously, Kayla scanned the heavens.

She had dismantled the navboard and com board

of the shuttle that Raintree and Fichu had used to follow her, taking some satisfaction in the job. The shuttle, she saw, was registered as belonging to Merrick, formerly the property of Pelleas Karlson. That bastard, she thought. He took everything that wasn't glued down. And that reminded her of some other unfinished business.

"Golias," she said. "Golias, get over here. I want to talk to you."

The dybbuk swung toward her.

"Mind telling me why you agreed to the deal that those agents suggested?"

"Deal?" "Keller's" eyes were blank.

"With Raintree and Fichu, remember? You were going to abandon us. Go off with them."

"Not abandon. Buy time."

"Yeah? You seemed pretty eager."

The dybbuk shrugged—or was that merely a shudder? Kayla suspected that she would get little more out of him. His powers of communication were still unreliable. And she didn't know what—if anything—he was likely to remember. But she didn't trust him. Couldn't.

Shivering, she looked up at the darkening sky. "Come on," she muttered. "Iger, get back here. It's getting cold."

Beside her "Keller" said nothing.

As dusk turned to night, the stars took on a

deeper, icy radiance. One pulled out of a cluster and moved toward them, flashing red and blue.

The *Antimony*'s shuttle.

It hovered for a moment, jets blowing the sand into miniature whirlwinds, and landed with a deep, resounding thump that rocked the beach. A small dune nearby collapsed.

Like a metal eye raising its lid, the air lock began to slide open. Kayla ran toward it and ducked in before it was more than half open, leaving the dybbuk to struggle through the sand as best he could.

"I thought you'd never get here," she said.

Iger leaned back in his webseat, grinning. "Think I'd just forget about you? No chance."

She gave him a quick hug, then moved to help "Keller" climb in and secure himself for the trip.

That accomplished, Kayla settled heavily into a webseat, strapped herself in, and said, "Let's get out of here. If I never see Bandar Sabya again I might be happy."

Iger took them up with all engines on full. Bandar Sabya receded, rapidly becoming a faint gray crescent lit only by starlight and the shuttle's jets.

Safely aloft, Iger checked the navboard and nodded. "*Antimony* in five minutes."

"How are they?" Kayla asked. "Salome and the others. How do they seem?"

"Wobbly. And still real suspicious."

"Still?? Well, I can't blame them. They've been through a bad time. And it's my fault."

"Don't be ridiculous. You were the only one who had any hope of getting us out of debt. It was risky, and they knew it. Business is always risky. And you took the biggest risk of all, getting sent onto that damned prison ship and busting out." He smiled. "I thought you were crazy."

She flashed him a brief grateful smile.

"*Antimony,*" he said. "Dead ahead."

"That was quick."

Iger punched in the ship's code, waited, frowned. "That's odd. *Really* odd."

"What's wrong?"

"She doesn't respond."

"Try again."

"Trying. Still nothing. I can't understand it, this worked perfectly when I was up here before." He leaned over and keyed the com board. "*Antimony, Antimony,* do you read?"

The answer came back in the grinding, mechanical tones of the knowbot. "Affirmative."

"Trigger air lock release, door A–4."

"Triggering."

But the doors to the *Antimony* stayed shut.

"Antimony," Iger said. "*Antimony,* respond. Trigger air lock release backup system."

"Sorry," came the familiar testy voice of Rab. "The knowbot seems to be malfunctioning."

"Rab, can you get those doors open?"

"Probably."

"What do you mean, probably? Get those open, dammit. We're running low on power."

"First," Rab said, "give us one good reason to trust you."

Chapter Ninteen

Kayla couldn't believe what she was hearing. Had Rab really lost his mind? He had to open the air lock and let them in before they lost power.

"Rab," Iger was saying. "Stop screwing around and open those locks!"

"That's not exactly a good reason."

"Rab! Rab, answer me."

But plead, cajole, and threaten as Iger would, there was no further response.

"Dammit," Kayal said. "I should have expected this. He's been acting strange since we found him."

Iger turned, outraged, to stare at her. "Expected lunacy? They've all been locked up in the dark for so long that they've completely lost their minds!"

"Not likely to regain them soon either." Kayla unstrapped herself and stood up carefully in the low gravity. "Is there a spaceworthy pressure suit on this bucket?"

"Check the aft bulkhead locker."

Kayla bounced along from handhold to handhold until she had reached the rear of the narrow passenger compartment. Hanging from one hand, she inserted thumb and forefinger into the locker trigger, and pressed.

The door sprang up and she saw two pressure suits and helmets folded neatly beside a jet pack.

"Guess I'm going for a space walk."

"I'll transmit the air lock code from screen to your suit's memory," Iger said.

"While you're at it, include the code to lock it open, too," Kayla said wryly. "I'd hate to go to all this trouble to get the door open just to have Rab come along behind me and slam it right in my face."

"Right. Okay. You've got it."

She slipped on the suit and set the helmet in place. The jet pack was a peculiar sensation in the middle of her back. Unsteadily, she made her way to the shuttle egress.

"Don't forget to lock your helmet."

Kayla held up a gloved hand and stepped into the ejector compartment. Depressed the lock lever.

Click.

She was whirled away from air, light, and warmth, all things human, and brought to a dark cold place where nothing lived. The smooth skin of the shuttle reflected the distant light of the stars. Kayla was standing—floating, really—beside the shuttle in hard vacuum.

Above and to her left was the *Antimony*, a glittering structure studded by dark solar collectors and set in bold relief against the mottled backdrop of the gas giant, Xenobe. Somewhere below was the moonlet St. Ilban. Or perhaps it was above. Directions in space were always confusing.

Kayla activated her jet pack.

The shuttle rolled away from her, or seemed to, and vertigo grabbed her. Which way was up? down? Stars everywhere and nowhere. She could drift here forever in the gravitational tides of Xenobe. A speck, smaller than the smallest comet.

But *Antimony* was almost within reach.

Another shot by the jets.

There.

Kayla reached out with a slow, swimming motion and caught a grapple framework halfway across the ship's belly. Pulled. She began to travel along the perimeter of the *Antimony,* below the viewscreen sensors.

It was slow, hard work to make her way toward the air locks, avoiding the gunports. She was sweating in her pressure suit before she saw the red air lock light winking gently at her.

Here goes, she thought. *Hope Iger's transmission was right*. She triggered the suit's memory and waited.

A row of green and yellow letters trailed briefly across her visor, blinked, disappeared.

The light above the air lock flashed. Turned blue.

Slowly the air lock doors began to slide apart.

Come on, Kayla thought. *Hurry up!*

With maddening slowness, the gap between the doors widened. Now it was wide enough to allow a human to pass, just barely. Heart pounding, Kayla clambered inside, half expecting to be met by one of her friends pointing a disruptor at her head.

The air lock bay was empty.

Kayla clung to a handhold and waited until the doors had slid completely into their housing.

Click.

Quickly she signaled Iger.

"All set. Get in here, fast!"

The shuttle approached, landing lights blinking.

Would Rab find a way to shut them down? Would he fire on Iger? Kayla couldn't imagine it: her old comrades turned deadly enemies. She couldn't bear to think about it. Wouldn't.

The shuttle loomed at the air lock.

Closer.

It nudged into the air lock like an egg moving back into its nest. The autograpples took it and brought it neatly home, snug in its grooved berth.

Kayla hit the manual override and the air lock doors slid closed on the terrifying darkness beyond.

The shuttle hatch sprang open. Iger smiled at her from the open doorway.

"That's doing it the hard way," he said. "Now all we have to do is take back *our* ship from *our* friends.

She nodded grimly. "Come on out. And bring the biggest guns you can find."

* * *

They moved slowly along the corridor, two armed figures poised to jump at any and every noise.

At least Salome and the others haven't noticed that we're here, yet, Kayla thought. *Or, if they have, they're not doing anything about it.*

And even as she thought that, the ship shuddered strangely. Engines came on, full-strength, roaring.

Kayla felt the familiar tug at her stomach and eyes, the light-headed dizziness that warned of imminent jump.

"Dammit," she said. "Iger, hang on, they're taking us into jumpspace!"

He gave her a quick, frightened look. "Jumpspace this close to a planet? Are they crazy? They'll go right through Xenobe and flatten us like choba dough!"

But there was no time to talk.

Space around them narrowed, then widened. The air seemed charged, fizzing with lethal energies.

The *Antimony* was in jumpspace, where every action created unexpected reactions.

"Where the hell are they taking us?" Iger said.

"God knows. Just sit tight and ride it out."

Kayla knew her way around jumpspace—knew, as well, that she could stop this crazy trip, could send a mental probe arrowing into Salome, who was doubtless piloting, and cause such convulsions that their trajectory would be interrupted. But it was terribly dangerous to interrupt a jump sequence. They might become trapped in the netherworld of jump-space, never to emerge, or be thrown across the galaxy and exit in a place they'd never seen before, from which they had no way of returning.

Best to ride along and deal with their friends when they once again emerged into realspace.

"Let's get back into the shuttle. It's safer there."

"Good idea."

Clinging together they made a slow retreat into the small craft and, with unsteady hands, strapped themselves down for the duration of the jump.

"Keller" was sitting quietly where they had left him, seemingly unaware of their new trajectory.

The *Antimony* shifted, bucked, went sideways and forward, all at the same time.

"Something's wrong," Kayla said. "This isn't the way jump is supposed to feel."

Before she could say more, the ship swung crazily, tilting, leaving shadows of itself in a sweeping path of nonrealtime. They were everywhere and nowhere, all at once.

"She's got to abort the jump," Kayla said. "No other choice now."

Sure enough, she could hear the jump engines winding their way down as the *Antimony* decelerated into realspace. It was a long, slow, dangerous process.

And then they were back in the galaxy, stopped dead.

"Iger, can you get anything on the shuttle screen?"

"Negative. Rab's got us shut down. No external input whatsoever, the bastard."

Kayla unstrapped herself and strode out of the shuttle. As she had suspected, the door of the shuttle bay was locked. She punched the intercom and, without waiting for a reply, began speaking. "Dammit, Rab, what's going on in ops?"

There was no response. Kayla wondered if the man was going to be totally stupid. "Need I point out that I'm your only other jump-qualified pilot? You want to tell me what the problem is or you want to drift here?"

Through what sounded like clenched teeth, Rab said, "Salome couldn't handle the strain. Fell apart as we passed a collapsing star: the gravity well grabbed us, but she managed to divert to another jump node. Then she caved in."

"So where are we?"

"I don't have a clue."

"Terrific," Kayla said. "Well, if you want to get out of here, you'd better let me into ops."

"Forget it."

"Look, Rab, I could shoot my way out of here, but I don't especially like the idea of firing a disruptor inside the *Antimony*. I don't think that you want me to do it either."

"You'll stay put, dammit. Salome will come 'round." His voice quavered for a moment. "When she does, we'll figure out where we are and go pick up the *Falstaff*."

"The *Falstaff*? Is that where you were headed? Where the hell is it?"

"Salabrian System."

"How did it get all the way over there?"

"Keller had it mothballed in the shipyards of Buffalo Port on Sala III. Or so he said."

Kayla put every ounce of persuasive power that she possessed into her voice. "Come on, Rab, let me take the board. You can ride it out with me and shut it down if you don't like what I'm doing. Hold a gun to my head the entire time if it makes you happy." Privately she hoped that he wouldn't take her up on the later part of that offer.

The only reply was the sound of the shuttle bay door, unlocking.

* * *

The room vanished and Kayla slid into the non-space of the jumpboard with its vivid geometric approximations of things: spiked purple towers, plunging yellow canyons, sheer slick walls. The vertiginous angles, the confusing perspective: she remembered it now. She had once spent subjective years of time in jumpspace. But not recently.

The glittering jump interface beckoned, beautiful as a waterfall and deadly to those unaccustomed to its twists, turns, sudden dead ends, and alleys.

I'll be ready for you in a few moments, Kayla thought. *But not just yet. Let me warm up first.*

She took the *Antimony* through some basic moves, reacquainting herself with the feel of the ship. It had more mass than the *Falstaff* and, with its bigger engines, was quicker to respond to her commands. Kayla savored the elegance of its response. The *Antimony* was a smoothly efficient flying machine that purred under her fingers.

The system in which they had landed wasn't much: a small, decaying white dwarf with three cold dead planetoids for company. Kayla parked the *Antimony* in wide orbit around the unknown sun: she could use its gravitational field in a slingshot effect to speed their journey. She set the knowbot to scanning the star maps for their location, plotting backward from the last known point and extrapolating the probable course Salome had taken to avoid the birthing black hole.

The knowbot took its time, scrolling through its backbrain. Finally, it beeped and unrolled the system's name onscreen in brilliant blue letters.

Gornik's Star.

Kayla had never heard of it. But the knowbot had,

and informed her that Salabria was a two-jump journey away. The coordinates were fed from the screen into the jumpboard. Now all Kayla had to do was find the jump node to begin their journey.

The engines came on and the knowbot triggered the automatic warning: "Jump in two minutes. Secure for jump. All hands secure. Two minutes."

Again Kayla felt the light-headed sensation, the tingling in her extremities that signaled imminent jump.

She hit the jump command and her stomach turned inside out on her.

The *Antimony* burst through the glittering interface waterfall and sped along winding shimmering canyons, making split-second turns and minute course adjustments. In jumpspace the ship was a giant red ball rolling madly, leaving streaks of light behind it, bouncing between jump nodes.

The second jump was coming up.

The *Antimony* skirted a series of candy-striped pillars, veered under an arch of flaming black squares, and pulled around a silvery pyramid tumbling end over end.

Attached by the black rubbery umbilici to the jumpboard, Kayla could feel the ship gathering itself for the jump.

"Five, four, three, two, one," droned the knowbot.

The waterfall again, the canyons, the careening turns and heart-stopping shifts.

But something else was there.

An anomaly. In jumpspace.

Kayla felt her heart thudding in her chest.

They could all die here.

One part of her mind wanted to pull back and analyze the situation. The other was busy plotting an evasive course.

The anomaly showed up on screen schematics: a lumpish accretion of mechanicals and thrusters. A dead ship, registry unknown, schematics unknown. A dead ship containing, most likely, a dead crew.

Kayla pulled a spiral course around the thing and avoided a collision. But in the process she missed the crucial exit node for Salabrian space.

Now the *Antimony* was flying blind in jump with no destination, no program.

Panic swelled up in her chest.

She had to find a deflection point, to attempt a return to the Salabrian node.

Black numerals and figures ghosted across her sight: the knowbot telling her, too late, that she had missed her turn. *Thanks a lot.*

Disorientation threatened to overwhelm her. Which way was up, which was down? She felt the coppery taste of fear in her mouth. No good. No time for that right now.

Quietly she disconnected Rab's override privilege. At least she didn't have to worry about him yanking her out of the jumpboard at a critical moment. She was in total control of the ship's trajectory now, for whatever good that might do.

Kayla walled off her fear and took a deep breath. She had to get them out of there.

A recalibration of jump points. That blue node, there, shaped like a melting wheel. And that node, whirling and spinning upon its pointed tip.

It would take a three-jump to return them to their exit point. A difficult maneuver. Kayla programmed the board and held her breath.

The *Antimony* shuddered and the jump engines whined. Kayla was tempted to just take the nearest jump node and exit, give the engines a rest, and forget the three-jump.

But where would we land? she wondered. *At least we know the way back from here.*

Got to do it now.

She set the coordinates and triggered the jumpboard again, holding on tightly.

Somewhere she was dimly aware of Rab trying furiously to stop her. She set the jumps on auto: even if he managed to knock her out, that wouldn't stop the ship.

Time was suspended as they floated from point to point. It was the most complicated course plotting that Kayla had ever done. Would it hold up? Would they find their way out of jumpspace?

First jump.

Second jump.

Third.

The lights dimmed and time slowed.

Gods, don't let us be caught in a feedback loop, Kayla prayed. *Please.*

They were moving through a wall of light like burning dust, scintillating with diamond particles.

The ship lights came up full power and the viewscreen showed a familiar backdrop of local galaxies. Dead ahead: the Salabrian System with its many planets and its red dwarf star glowing like a ruby against velvet.

Kayla uttered a thankful sigh and put them in orbit around Sala III. All she wanted now was a chance to rest, to check on Third Child, and perhaps down a glass of Red Jack.

She pulled off the jumpboard connectors and ops sprang back into being around her.

Rab stood nearby. In his hands was a laser pistol as big as his head.

"Goddamn it, Rab!" Kayla's temper ignited. Careless of her peril, she got to her feet and faced her towering adversary. "I am bloody well tired of your suspicions. I nearly died for you once, in Vardalia, remember? To save your life I damaged my own mindpowers, permanently. But I guess that's not good enough for you. So shoot me and get it over with." She paused. "Well?"

Rab looked confused and frustrated. He stared from left to right, but there was no help coming from the inert Salome or the knowbot. "I gotta know," he said hoarsely. "Did you do it? Did you run out on us?"

"No, Rab. You disappeared and I've been searching for you ever since."

"Swear on your parents' deaths." His gaze pinned her to the floor.

"All right. On their deaths."

Nobody made a sound. Rab held the gun on her for a moment longer. Then something shifted behind his eyes. He lowered the pistol. "Well, all right then."

Arsobades wasn't as easily satisfied, nor was Salome when she came around.

"Katie," said the *Falstaff*'s captain. "I don't care what Rab thinks. You're a traitor."

"Bullshit," Kayla snapped. "I won't accept that, Salome. You're just looking for somebody to blame."

"That's an easy rationalization."

"I could have stopped you from taking the *Antimony*—or even trying. But I knew that I could hurt you with my mindpowers, so I didn't. And then I saved your ass when you collapsed."

"You left us to rot in that jail!"

"That's not true. I didn't know what had happened to you. And when I found out, I did everything I could to find you. But it took some time."

"Convenient. While you racked up a fortune."

"You're completely crazy," Kayla said. "Where's my fortune? Where's my wealth?"

"You were so crazy for that frigging Mindstar—"

"I wanted it for *us*, Salome. For the *Falstaff*, remember? To get us out of hock."

"All I know is you went running off after that mindstone and we ended up rotting in that hole. I thought we'd die there."

"And to get revenge you tried to leave me—and Iger—in an even worse position than the way that you think I left you."

"What do you mean?"

"Oh, come off it. You were trying to strand us in space. Low on fuel. You know that we'd have suffocated. Shooting us would have been kinder."

"You could have found us, Katie. You could have used your famous mindpowers." Salome made a face as though the words left a bad taste in her mouth.

"You give me too much credit," Kayla said. "I don't have those sorts of powers anymore. Lost them years ago and you know it. You know how, too. But you're so determined to hate me—when you should be thanking me for freeing you, and saving you just now—that you think my failure to find you sooner is some sort of treachery."

Arsobades gave her a look that was half belligerance and half shame. "You try spending a year in prison and see how well you like it, Katie."

"Goddammit, I did! Spent enough time behind bars to leave its taste in the back of my mind forever. And I did it for the good of my ship and my friends—at least, I thought you were my friends. I've risked my life for you and the *Falstaff* plenty of times. But I'm tired of arguing. You want to blame me? Fine. You say that the *Falstaff* is moored here in the shipyards? Go get it. At the very least, get the hell off my ship."

Rab's expression had softened. He held out a huge hand to her. "Katie, wait—"

"No, Rab. Take the *Falstaff.* You're free. Safe. Maybe the only way I can prove myself to you is to set you free, leave you alone." She was aware of something aching at the back of her eyes and throat but she shoved the awareness down savagely. "I'm going back to St. Ilban with Iger and Third Child."

"And Keller." The implication hung there between them.

"Yes, and Keller. Or, rather, Keller's body. But I'm not going to explain that to you again either."

"Katie—"

"Save it, Rab. I hope I'll see you all again someday."

One by one her former comrades filed silently out of ops. She watched them go, not saying a word more.

Chapter Twenty

Vardalia was a city holding its breath.

With good reason.

Merrick the Blackbird and his forces had checkmated Lyle MacKenzie, Darius Peters, and the police of Vardalia. At stake was control of the city.

So far, neither side had blinked. But the impasse couldn't last. When one side eventually moved, the struggle that would follow promised to be long, bitter, and bloody.

* * *

In a sharply sour mood Kayla brought the *Antimony* out of jumpspace and into the Cavinas System. Past Styx, quickly, and tawny Liage, and finally into the gravitational tides of Xenobe and its moon, St. Ilban.

The twin stars of Cavinas twinkled at the heart of the system, yellow and green, constant companions.

But Kayla wouldn't have been surprised to see them go supernovae on the instant.

Nothing is forever, she thought grimly. *Nothing lasts. Not stars. Not friendships. Not galaxies.*

Vardalia Port gave them berth without difficulty.

Kayla put the ship on autodock and review. "Come on, Iger," she said. "I've got some questions I want to ask Merrick. And if I don't like his answers, I'm going to tack his ugly hide above the door of the Crystal Palace."

* * *

The rooms in the Crystal Palace glowed with a new-found luster. Every reflective surface had been buffed to mirrorlike perfection. The tapestries and draperies were immaculate. Merrick the Blackbird surveyed his apartment with immense satisfaction and brushed a microscopic piece of dust from the top of a spiraling iridescent vase.

"Have some more punch, Cris," he offered, playing the genial host. The fluted crystal glass he handed Cristobal held a potent combination of fruit nectars and mindsalt. He wanted Cristobal to be as pliant as possible. "Drink up."

Cristobal grasped the goblet, saluted Merrick with it, and downed its frothy contents in two gulps.

The drug took effect almost immediately, dilating his pupils and giving his face a slack, inattentive cast.

"Sit down," Merrick said.

Cristobal sat.

"What have you learned about Raintree and Fichu?"

When Cristobal answered, his words were slurred as though he didn't have full control of his tongue. "Nothing. They've disappeared. Taken that shuttle and gone over the edge of the world. Fallen off."

"Well, good riddance, although I hate to lose valuable equipment. But a shuttle can be replaced. And so can they."

"Here, here." Cristobal held up his glass for a refill.

Merrick took it from him but instead of filling it full of mindsalt brew, he grinned and placed it in the recycler. "That's enough for now," he said.

The Blackbird paused to light up a smoke stick and took a long drag on it. Savored it, nodding. Then exhaled a cloud of fluorescent green smoke and said, "What about Mac? Have you been keeping track of his movements?"

"Sure. Not that I can do very much about getting anywhere near him. There are so many police around him that he looks like a damned parade."

Merrick waved the complaint away. "You're just not being creative, Cris. Don't try to come at it head-on. Check out all sorts of different angles. Something's bound to occur. You'll find your opportunity." The Blackbird might have been discussing painting technique with a young apprentice. He nodded encouragingly. "Not to worry."

"Yeah? What about Darius Peters? What about all that police protection?"

"Even Darius Peters' resources have their limitations. I suppose that we'll just have to see that they're overextended." And Merrick began to laugh. After a moment, Cristobal obediently joined in.

* * *

Only Kayla and Iger ventured into Vardalia from the port. The last thing that Kayla wanted was to be burdened by a pregnant dalkoi and a zombie barely in control of its body, especially if she had to move fast.

They rang at Lyle MacKenzie's safe house. A pleasant-faced woman in military garb answered the door and, after they presented ID, directed them to MacKenzie's new location in the heart of Vardalia's Musicians' Quarter. It was a simple, two-story, whitewashed building. An armed guard admitted them.

Kayla discovered to her surprise that MacKenzie wasn't alone. His visitors included Darius Peters and a small, dark-haired woman, beautiful and exquisitely dressed, who clung close, very close, to Darius Peters.

"Katie," MacKenzie said. "Back again and this

time for good, I hope. You know Minister Peters of course. And this is Ti-ling, his companion."

Kayla nodded. She found herself taking an instant dislike to the sleek little woman.

Soft and protected, this one. Nestled like a cat at Darius Peters' side, casting smug glances up at him. Kayla wanted to kick her. Hadn't this Ti-lung once been Pelleas Karlson's mistress? Yes, of course she had. Well, just look at her. What else was she good for?

She had the pampered air of a privileged pet. The condescending look she flashed at the spacers did nothing to improve Kayla's opinion. The companions of the powerful often got jumped-up ideas about their own importance.

Kayla felt impatient, then angry with the woman, and by extension, all cosseted planet dwellers, those people who had the luxury to be naive, to be safe and protected, to make assumptions about their continued safety . . . and innocence. Who had no experience of the greater galaxy, no experience of prisons. Of young girls crying hopelessly in the night. They had heard gunshots in the distance, once, perhaps, and shivered with the delicious awareness that they were safe in the midst of danger, and decided that they had experienced a thrilling bit of real life.

They had no idea what real danger was. But they just might find out.

"So, Katie," MacKenzie said, bursting into her

thoughts. "You found Salome and the others? Safe and sound?"

"Yes." She didn't bother to conceal the minor note in her voice, the sad look on her face.

MacKenzie frowned at her, but she ignored the obvious question in his eyes. She didn't intend to explain. "They're all aboard the *Falstaff.*"

"The ship? Where'd they find it?"

"Picked it up at Buffalo Port."

"And when will we be seeing them?"

"I don't know."

MacKenzie's hazel eyes widened in surprise. But he said nothing. Nodding slowly, he turned to Peters. "Let's table the meeting, Darius, all right? I'll see you tomorrow."

The Police Minister nodded and began to rise. But just as he did his portacom began buzzing. He pulled it from his belt and flipped it open. "Peters."

The face of Lt. Commander Sherno appeared onscreen. "Sir, you'd better get back to headquarters." His voice could be heard throughout the room.

"What's happening?" Peters demanded.

"A bomb went off at the District Four armory."

Peters scowled. "How bad?"

"Three dead. The place is in ruins. And there's a major disturbance going on in District Six."

"The Beggars' Quarter?"

"It's engulfed the entire Quarter already and is

threatening to spread well beyond. Looks to us as if outside agitation started it up."

"And we know who that is," Peters rumbled. "That bastard, Merrrick. Sherno, get as many people over there just as fast as you can."

Sherno said, "Three people are dead already. They won't be the last."

"I'm on my way."

"Sounds ugly," said MacKenzie.

"Mac, you stay put," Peters said. "Ti-ling, I'll drop you off at home on the way."

"But, Darius, I want to be with you."

He gestured impatiently. "Don't be silly."

With a rustle of silk the tiny woman was out the door, leaving a wake of fine perfume.

Peters paused on the doorstep. "Stay safe, folks." With a nod, he was gone.

MacKenzie sat down heavily. His wiry frame, never very fleshy, had gone to skin and bones during his recuperation. "We are going to have to do something," he said, staring at Kayla and then at Iger. "Something about Merrick the Blackbird."

"He's behind this?" Iger asked.

"He's behind everything," MacKenzie said. "Everything that stinks in Vardalia."

"And elsewhere," Kayla added. "We found Salome, Rab, and Arsobades penned up in a hellhole on Bandar Sabya. While we were rescuing them, guess who turns up? Two of Merrick's agents. They followed us in a shuttle that the Blackbird owns. It all adds up, doesn't it?"

"What's that bastard after?" Iger said. "Power?"

"That," said MacKenzie. "And wealth. And he wouldn't turn down the mindsalt trade either."

"In other words, he wants it all."

Kayla sighed. "And he's definitely upped the stakes if he's begun to set off bombs in different districts."

"Which means that he's ready to destroy it," MacKenzie said. "If he can't have Vardalia, then nobody can. The man is pathologically greedy."

"Well, I've got something in mind that might surprise him," Kayla said. She smiled sourly. "Something he won't be expecting."

* * *

The *Antimony* rode easily at anchor, tucked into its berth, attached to the dock by fuel umbilicals that could be sliced away in an emergency.

Inside the ship was quiet, the only sound that of the mech-systems making their checks, the relays clicking, working down the length of ops.

Third Child slept deeply, curled into her bunk, toes twitching gently.

The dybbuk "Keller" sat alone in the darkened room. What he was thinking—or if he *was* thinking—

was impossible to know. His face was slack, expressionless. The eyes seemed lifeless.

"Golias?" Kayla said.

For a moment the dybbuk didn't respond.

"Golias, answer me!"

Slowly the head lifted, the eyes swiveled in their sockets. "Kayla."

One by one the hairs on the back of her neck stood up. Golias rarely called her by that name. She had usually been "Katie" to him. But Keller had called her Kayla. Whose brain was really animating that body?

"Golias, listen carefully. I have a job for you. An important one."

"Job?"

Suspicion roiled in her. Was this Golias, looking at her through Yates Keller's eyes? Or was Keller himself beginning somehow to glide back up into consciousness? "A job, yes. But first I'd like you to answer some questions."

"All right."

"Tell me who Shotay was."

"Shotay." The dybbuk paused and its attention seemed to withdraw back within its own skull.

Kayla waited, watching carefully.

A spark had ignited within the dead eyes. "Keller" stirred. "Shotay, yes. Sister. My sister. She was your friend. You tried to protect her but you couldn't. She died in prison." The spark went out.

He had hit all of the right points, she couldn't fault him. "Yes," she said. "Good. Now, about this job. I want you to go see Merrick for me."

"Merrick the Blackbird? Why?"

"Because you're the last thing that he'd look for." Kayla leaned closer, fighting the surge of revulsion that she felt. "I want you to go in there and convince him that you're really, truly Yates Keller. And that you want to cut him in on the biggest deal of his life."

"What's that?"

Kayla took a deep breath. "The *Falstaff*."

"Keller" nodded and a ghost of a smile curved the corners of his mouth. "Tell me more."

* * *

After "Keller" had embarked upon his mission, Kayla joined Iger in the *Antimony*'s ops and explained her plan.

"The *Falstaff*?" Iger stared at her. "Have you gone completely space-batty? Merrick is a greedy son of a bitch. Why would he care about that creaky old tub when there's an entire planet's worth of riches sitting right here beneath his nose, just waiting his plunder?"

With the exaggerated patience that she usually reserved for idiots, Kayla carefully explained. "He wants the *Falstaff*. Always has. For a time he even thought tht he was in love with Salome, but he was just kidding himself. It was her ship that he wanted, not Salome."

"Merrick has the hots for the ship?" Iger sounded more confused than before.

"You know that Salome inherited the ship from her uncle. And Merrick knows it, too. He thinks that the *Falstaff* has two generations' worth of data stored in the knowbot's backbrain. All kinds of stuff about all the hidden fortunes in the Three Systems, and beyond."

Iger's expression turned apprehensive. "Does it?"

"The *Falstaff*'s knowbot?" Kayla rolled her eyes. "Get real. That thing can't even tell the time out of the Cavinas System. It's incredibly primitive. Besides, if Salome had that kind of information at her fingertips, do you think she would ever have wasted even a minute on my plan about the Mindstar?"

"Good point. But are you sure it makes sense to send that dybbuk to fool Merrick? Katie, he can barely walk a straight line. Asking him to impersonate Keller is just asking for trouble."

"Let's just wait and see."

Chapter Twenty-One

The public rooms of Merrick's apartment tinkled with the sound of wind chimes, but the mood was far from tranquil.

"You?" Cristobal swept back against the gem-studded wall until the model of Styx was poking him squarely in mid-spine. "You're dead. You can't be here, you can't."

The dybbuk "Keller" stepped closer. "Hello, Cristobal."

"You're dead. I saw your ship go up near Styx."

"Must have been somebody else."

"No." Cristobal's mouth worked. "I'm dreaming. I must be asleep. This is a nightmare."

"Keller" reached forward.

"Don't touch me! Don't hurt me. I did what you asked, didn't I? I blew Brayton's Rock. Killed all those people." He staggered a bit, rubbing his eyes. "All those people . . ."

"Where's Merrick?"

"You don't care about me! You use people and then you drop them when you're finished."

"Where's Merrick?"

"Damn you!" Cristobal's expression had twisted from grief to anger. "Pay attention to me."

"I want Merrick."

"Oh, Merrick, Merrick, everybody always wants Merrick!"

"Is he in?"

Cristobal's eyes glinted suddenly. "Take me back under your protection."

The dybbuk raised its arm as if to bat Cristobal out of its way.

A sudden whisper of silk, a hint of musky perfume. Ti-ling stood in the doorway, watching the two men. "Oh, forgive me." Her voice was low and insinuating. "I was looking for Merrick."

The dybbuk swung toward her. "Where is he? I want to find him, too."

"Keller?" Ti-ling's eyes widened. "Yates Keller, that's who you are, right? Or who you were. I heard about what happened to you on Styx . . ."

"What is all this racket?" Merrick emerged from an inner room, his dark hair tousled from sleep. He surveyed the group sourly, pausing when he came to "Keller." *"You?"* Every vestige of sleepiness disappeared.

Cristobal made a sound in his throat like a frightened animal and bolted out the door.

"Keller. Son of a bitch. I didn't think you'd be coming back," Merrick said. "But it looks like you're here. Gods, man, I should kill you. You know you busted me."

"Did I?"

"Don't play innocent with me. You know what you did. You think I would have turned to these rebels otherwise? And now that I'm in the catbird seat, you show up and want it all back? No way, Keller!" He loomed over the dybbuk. "You were the big deal here before, but it's all changed now. And you won't get it back, not without a fight."

Ti-ling stepped forward. "Merrick, this isn't who you think it is . . ."

He waved her to silence. "You're finished here, Keller. Might as well get on the next shuttle to Salabria."

Frantically Ti-ling tried to get his attention, but Merrick implacably ignored her.

A buzzer cut into the discussion.

"Yeah?" Merrick snapped.

A voice came out of an onyx speaker. "There's something down here at the spaceport, boss, something that you should see."

"Like what?"

"Like a ship's hold filled with mindsalt."

"Whose ship?"

"*Clown Princess.* Registered to one Roger Bad-Eye Collins. Deceased."

"Deceased? How recently?"

"This morning. The riot in the Beggars' Quarter. He was looking the wrong way at the wrong time."

"Hmm. All right. You say it's filled with mindsalt?"

"To the very tiptop."

"Let's have that ship registry transferred, pronto."

"No good. The heirs are already clamoring for it."

"Then get that shipment moved. That's the last mindsalt in the city that I know of."

"Yeah. Well, you'd better get some people down here, fast. The heirs are on their way."

"Stall 'em."

"You better make sure that you cut me in on this deal."

"Bastard!" Merrick hesitated. "All right. Just don't let them at that salt!"

* * *

Kayla leaned back in her webseat in *Antimony*'s ops and pulled the plug out of her ear with deep satisfaction. Turning to Iger, she said: "Get all that?"

"Every word."

"Damn! Good thing I wired Golias with a mech-ear."

"So that Ti-ling is working for Merrick and sleeping with Peters." Iger shook his head.

"I knew I didn't like that bitch. And Darius Peters

isn't going to be pleased to hear that his girlfriend is double-crossing him. Not at all."

"Shouldn't that wait until you report the mindsalt shipment?" Iger said.

"I'm not going to report it."

"No?"

"I'm going to go one better, and steal it."

"Steal it?" He gave her a look of complete confusion. "Why?"

"That'll give me a negotiating wedge with Merrick."

"I don't think we should negotiate with that one," Iger said. "I think we should put a sack over his head and drop him out the nearest air lock."

Kayla gave him a tight smile. "And I'm supposed to be the bloodthirsty one around here." She shook her head in mock disapproval. "Come on."

* * *

Three groups converged upon the freighter: the less-than-grief-stricken heirs of Bad-Eye Collins, Merrick and "Keller," and Kayla.

Merrick's agent at the dock held the Collins group at bay as Merrick began to slip past them.

But one woman in the crowd, sleek-haired, tan, with glinting metal teeth, grabbed Merrick's cape and screamed," I know what you're up to, Blackbird. I know what you want. But you can't get past me!"

"Goddamn you, bitch, let go of me!" Merrick slapped out at her but somehow the woman hung on, evading his blows. "Keller, get her off of me," Merrick yelled.

The dybbuk lumbered forward.

The woman lashed out at "Keller" with an elegantly shod foot and kicked him in the knee.

"Keller" recoiled and staggered back, a look of confusion on his face.

As Merrick swatted at the woman, Kayla crept out of her hiding place. She could see a group of police approaching with Lt. Commander Sherno in the lead.

The noisy crowd boiled over and around itself, quite oblivious to the contested but unguarded cruiser.

Moving faster, Kayla bounded up the access tube, broke the seal on the *Clown Princess'* air lock, and clambered aboard.

A small ship that had seen hard use, the *Princess* was nothing to fight over as far as Kayla could see. Its board casings were cracked, its hull coat worn to dull metal in the doorways and around the wall holds.

She heard loud noises near the air lock—Merrick and the heirs bringing their fight for possession closer. There wasn't a moment to lose.

She found ops easily. It was small work to plug into the navboard umbilicals. A switch here, a nudge there. Lights flickered, machinery muttered, and the engines came to life. Their roar filled the cabin.

This old tub needs a tune-up, Kayla thought. But the sound of those engines might just serve to clear the air lock.

Onscreen she saw Bad-Eye Collins' family milling near the gate to the tube gantry. She couldn't spot Merrick in the crowd—that was bad news. Probably meant that he was already in the air lock access tube. And where was "Keller"? The thought of him on the loose left her uneasy.

She scanned the ship and saw to her dismay that three other life-forms had boarded. Quickly Kayla locked and secured ops.

The com board buzzed: Port Authority demanding that she shut down. *Not a chance,* she thought.

Kayla put through a call of her own. "Port Authority," she said. "Clear the air lanes. I'm taking the *Clown Princess* up, emergency liftoff."

Klaxons howled their warning as the Port readied itself for catastrophe. Fire walls slammed down between berths, emergency mechs extruded from the ceilings and floors, and all nonessential port functions were frozen or cut off.

Kayla instructed the knowbot to commence countdown for ignition, then contacted Port Authority again. "Vardalia Port: you have two minutes to clear the area."

On the viewscreen figures could be seen desperately scrambling for cover.

Port Authority buzzed the com board until, to cut the noise, Kayla disabled the circuit.

"Three. Two. One. Ignition!"

She took the ship up, hard, all engines on full.

The *Clown Princess* bucked and whined. A sensor began blinking, indicating a stress fracture in number three hold. Kayla checked it quickly: it wasn't a main support. She sent mechs scurrying to apply a plasteel brace.

The intensified g-force shoved Kayla back and down into the webseat. She knew that anybody left standing on the ship had been knocked to the floor by the increased gravitational pull of the accelerating ship.

Up, up, up.

Vardalia Port barely got the dome doors open in time. The *Clown Princess* went roaring through them, clearing the dome with scant inches to spare.

Up through the clouds, up through the atmosphere toward purple Xenobe. Then a quick course change and the cruiser dropped into orbit around St. Ilban.

Kayla scanned the ship again. Sure enough, holds one and two were filled with mindsalt. She saw to her chagrin that Merrick had indeed made it aboard before takeoff. That left two other life-forms unaccounted for. Wait. There. "Keller" had somehow gotten aboard, too, and was stumbling along on the lower deck. The third man was Lt. Commander Sherno, located halfway between the air lock and ops. Kayla hoped that Sherno managed to reach her before Merrick did.

Amber warning lights began blinking on the boards. The ship was definitely showing the strain of its sudden leap into space.

Loud pounding filled the room. Somebody was battering at the locked ops door.

"Let me in! Open it."

Merrick.

"Bash away all you want," Kayla said. "Pound to your heart's content, you bastard."

"Dammit, I'm going to get that mindsalt."

"Not if I can help it, you aren't."

Kayla peered at the navboard. There was something odd about the track that the *Princess* was following. She saw a yellow worry-light winking frantically on the board, but she couldn't locate the problem.

Szzzit!

It was the sound of a laser, burning through ceramsteel. The bulkhead. Merrick was cutting his way into ops.

Kayla grabbed her disruptor and checked its power levels. Ready.

"Come on," she muttered. "I'm waiting." Where was Sherno? Had Merrick surprised him? Killed him?

A jagged line, red and glowing, began to etch its way up the wall near the door to ops. When it was barely, just barely, the height of a tall man, the line swung around and began to snake downward. As Kayla watched, the burning arc reached the floor-plates and went black. With a hissing sigh, the area of wall contained within the ragged outline fell toward Kayla and clattered upon the floor of ops.

Behind, in the corridor, stood Merrick, a pistol glowing in his fist.

Kayla raised her disruptor.

—*See you in hell, Blackbird.*

The ship kicked and, engines whining, skewed violently. Ops vibrated as though it were a bell whose clapper had just struck a violent note.

Merrick lost hold of his laser pistol and it went flying across the room.

Kayla tumbled over the navboard, pulling loose from the umbilicals to fetch up against the bulkhead.

"What the hell?" Merrick shouted. He began to bounce slightly, his black cloak rippling with strange eddies.

Alarms were ringing, faintly.

The ship's artificial gravity had failed.

In the slow-motion of low-g, hand over hand, Kayla pulled herself back to the main board.

What she saw was a navigator's nightmare: a maze of blinking lights: every board in sight was lit up like a night in wicked old Vardalia, flashing "crisis, crisis!" The ship had blown its master system. The controls were useless.

Kayla couldn't navigate. The com board was dead. She couldn't even call for help.

"Get to the escape pod!" she shouted. "The ship's destabilizing. Gravity's going. We've got to abandon this tub before it kills us."

"Not without the salt," said Merrick.

"Are you crazy?"

"This is just a trick, isn't it?" the Blackbird asked angrily. "Some nifty trick to keep me from getting the mindsalt. But it isn't going to work!" He flailed out and, with a meaty hand, gave her a powerful shove.

Kayla went tumbling up against the far wall. There she managed to snag a wall hold and right herself. "Merrick," she said. "I don't care what cockeyed fantasy you may have about what's going on here. I'm getting myself to the escape pod before the environmental controls fail, too."

"Where's the salt?"

"In holds one and two. You're welcome to it, if you can figure out how to get down there. Have fun. Have yourself a party!"

The lights went out.

A few seconds later—an eternity in the dark—a greenish light, bilious and eerie, came flickering up from the floorplates. At least, the ship's backup glowglobes were still operational.

She and Merrick began a slow-motion chase in the green-tinged dark of the dying ship. Pushing off bulkheads to float slowly—maddeningly slowly—through the thickening air, Kayla stayed a precious few steps ahead of the Blackbird. The air recyclers had cut off. Soon, Kayla knew, the air aboard ship would be unbreathable. She had to get herself to a pressure suit and then to an escape pod.

Hand over hand, she pulled herself along the wall, searching for the suit locker.

Suddenly a hand reached out of the dark and caught her by the arm. She struggled in its grasp. Looking up she saw the dead face of "Keller" staring at her, starkly lit in profile by the green emergency lights.

"Golias, let go of me!"

There was no response. Again suspicion raced through Kayla: was the mindghost still operating Keller's body—or had Keller somehow regained consciousness and succeeded in ejecting his ghostly hitchhiker?

"Golias!" Using mindpower alone she jolted him back against the wall, slamming him hard. His grip relaxed and she slithered out of his hands.

"Don't release her, fool! Hold her!" Merrick came bouncing into range but Kayla was already down the corridor pulling herself along and praying for a jet pack.

"Hsst! Ms. Shadow, over here."

Lt. Commander Sherno held a hand out of a compartment, beckoning.

He was wearing a pressure suit and holding another.

Kayla didn't ask questions. Nodding her thanks, she donned the suit as quickly as possible, moving clumsily in the low-g.

"Freeze."

Merrick stood behind them, a dark shape filling the corridor. There was just enough light to see that he held a laser pistol aimed directly at Kayla.

Sherno shoved her behind him. "Merrick," he said. "Drop the gun. You're under arrest."

"Arrest?" The Blackbird lowered the pistol and gaped at the patrolman in obvious disbelief. His voice crackled with amusement. "On what charges?"

"Dealing in contraband goods. Attempted assault with intent to murder." Sherno paused, frowning. "I've got the other charges on my portascreen." He patted his pockets, then shrugged. "Back in Vardalia Port."

Now Merrick laughed loud and long. "We're not on St. Ilban, Sherno. You're just a city cop. You have no authority up here. Nice try, though." He raised his pistol again.

"Wait," Kayla cried.

Two things happened.

Merrick fired. But the dybbuk "Keller" grabbed

him at the same time and the shot went wild, taking out part of the wall near the air lock.

With a quiet pop, the lock blew and the ship's atmosphere began to stream out into space.

Chapter Twenty-Two

The weather conditions aboard the *Clown Princess* underwent alarming changes as gale winds generated by the sudden pressure drop swept everything before them toward the damaged air lock. Caught up in the storm, Kayla grabbed desperately for a wall hold and hung on for her life.

Like a great black bird Merrick soared past her toward the opening in the ship's wall. For a moment he caught the edges of the door, spread-eagled, his face contorting from pressure and oxygen loss. Then, soundlessly, he was gone, a black shape whose edges fluttered against the mist that conveyed him into the deeper blackness waiting beyond.

Kayla watched in silent anguish. She had no love for the man, but to suffocate in space, unprotected, was a particularly ugly death, a spacer's nightmare.

Right behind Merrick flew "Keller," his arms and legs flailing in slow circles.

As he went past her, Kayla caught his arm and

pulled, hard. He began to move in her direction. But he didn't have a pressure suit. How would he survive in the near-vacuum within the ship?

She scanned the equipment nearby. There. Enclosed within a man-sized transparent box, an emergency oxygen/pressure feed. "Keller" could plug himself into the wall unit until she could get a seal on the air lock and find him a pressure suit.

—*Thanks,* Golias said, his mindspeech faint but surprisingly steady.

Kayla froze. She was in sudden unexpected linkage with the mindghost, seeing what he saw, thinking what he thought. Her mind rebelled at the information coming from two sets of eyes. Kayla closed hers.

She saw, through Golias' mind, in Keller's memory, a table of mindstones, shining red-blue-bronze. A vid cube full of instructions on how to cut each stone to use its mind-altering properties.

Now Golias knew where the stones were. Knew, too, how to cut them, how to use them, how to form and use groupminds.

The mindghost was gaining more and more access to Yates Keller's memories as he mastered the use of his body.

But what if Keller's residual personality came, in time, to dominate Golias? He would become Keller twice over. Twice as deadly, twice as ruthless.

Remember, Kayla warned herself, *Golias started as a*

criminal, willing to sell his own sister's body for profit. What would a Golias/Keller dual mind be capable of?

At the moment she thought it, Golias thought it, too. He saw the awareness dawning within her and began to protest.

—No! It won't be like that. You'll see.

—Golias. I can't take that chance.

His eyes were wide with terror. *—But it's cold-blooded murder. And I saved you and Sherno from Merrick.*

—Yes.

—You can't do it.

—You've had more chances at life than most, Golias. I can't expose people to the risk of you. It's my responsibility.

—Playing God now?

—Maybe. I hope not.

—Do you want more blood on your hands?

—What I want doesn't matter.

Kayla stared at him through the faceplate of her pressure suit, knowing what she had to do. Quickly, before she lost her nerve.

Kayla opened her hand.

The laws of physics did the rest.

"Keller" was caught up like a leaf in a windstorm, whirled in circles across the corridor and through the damaged air lock into the void.

—Murderer! Sister Blood. You're really Sister Blood!

Savagely, Kayla severed the mindlink. But Golias'

furious cry echoed in her skull. For long moments she hung in the crippled ship's hallway, eyes closed, the import of what she had done resonating through her like a cold drumbeat.

Decompression increased. A wallplate tore loose and sailed past.

She opened her eyes.

The pull of space was insistent, immense. Kayla felt her grip slipping. *I'm next,* she thought. *First Merrick, then Keller, and now me.*

Not far from her, Lt. Commander Sherno dangled from a wallhold. As Kayla watched in horror, the handle pulled free of the fractured wallplate and Sherno began a slow tumble toward the gaping air lock.

Kayla grabbed for his foot, snagged it, and held on. She couldn't let him be dragged out of the ship. But every movement was so slow, so difficult, like swimming through deep water.

Even as she tried to draw Sherno away from the air lock, Kayla lost her own grip and slid from her perch. Clinging helplessly to Sherno's foot, she was pulled with him out of the green darkness of the ship and into the starlit vacuum.

For a time they kept pace with the *Clown Princess,* helpless satellites, until a silent explosion vented the remainder of the *Princess'* atmosphere, and with it, two holds' worth of mindsalt. A shimmering pink-green-bronze cloud haloed the ship before its momentum carried it deeper into space, scattering and dissipating the sparkling particles.

The *Princess* fell away from them, or seemed to, accelerating toward the purple bulk of Xenobe.

Kayla swam closer to Sherno and peered into his helmet. His eyes, wide and hopeless, stared back. He made a movement that might have been a shrug, but the confines of the pressure suit made it impossible to tell. She tried to reach him with mindspeech but had no luck in making contact.

Silent, they hung together between the planets. The atmosphere within their suits would keep them alive for a time. But then that, too, would give out.

Kayla gazed around her at the place where she was going to die.

It was beautiful.

The Cavinas System and its planets whirled in their stately slow-motion ballet: the small ruby ball of Styx in the outer darkness, blond glowing Liage, the prairie world, and great purple Xenobe with her consort, St. Ilban, all of them in thrall to the twin suns of the Cavinas System.

Again and again Kayla's eyes returned to Styx, world of her birth, source of so many sorrows. *Look at it there,* she thought. *A cold red ball of rock. The universe is full of cold rocks circling suns, and their cold, sad stories. What does it mean? What does it really mean?*

Staring at the implacable geometries of the galaxy,

Kayla realized that she understood very little of what was important, about what mattered.

Life. Love. Connection. They were the only points of warmth in the wide, chill universe.

You can't chase your past forever, she thought, *can't spend your life trying to right wrongs done to you. What's done is done. Life is short. Savor it. Savor the moment.*

But this was a moment that was rather difficult to savor—with Death right around the next asteroid, just waiting for her air to run out.

So ends Sister Blood.

It's so quiet. I wish I could talk to Iger.

And tears came to her eyes at the thought of her lover, strong and graceful Iger, loyal and uncomplaining. She hadn't had a chance to say good-bye, to tell him that she loved him. And now it was too late.

A light flared suddenly, a diamond flower blooming against black velvet. A comet? A supernova? And over there, the faint, wavering tendrils of a gas nebula, floating like a phosphorescent jellyfish in the depths of the galaxy.

Nothing above and stars beneath her feet.

The vastness of spaces and forces beyond her comprehension. Her own tiny problems, her fears, joys, blood-feuds, shrank to insignificance here.

Kayla floated in the starlit dark, feeling sad and giddy at the same time. The universe was so beautiful, so filled with mystery and delight. But she was going to die. Her thoughts looped around in arcs. Her air was running out.

Clinging beside her, Sherno could have been a million miles away for all the communication that was possible between them. Still, his presence was a comfort. His presence, and that of the radiant stars.

One star detached itself and moved closer.

Her air readout was on zero.

She was in a dark passage, but there was a light up ahead. Were those angels waiting? Kayla went toward the light.

"What the hell are you up to?" said a familiar, beloved, rasping voice. "Get your ass in here. And who's your friend?"

Home, she was home. And there were arms to welcome her, to take her in.

* * *

The mood in Darius Peters' office was grim.

Iger watched the information scrolling down the screen and, for a shocked and frozen moment, his mind refused to believe what he had just seen.

Katie dead? Dead and gone?

Sorrow threatened to squash him flat. He fought it, bit his tongue to hold back the sobs certain to come. It couldn't be true. Katie wasn't dead.

Not until he said so.

Behind him, Peters and Lyle MacKenzie read the same data and exchanged quick, anxious looks.

Iger couldn't hold back the tide any longer. Knuckling a tear away as it slid past his nose, he said, "The ship's gone, with all hands."

"You're positive?" MacKenzie demanded.

Iger wanted to throttle him. "According to this report, the *Clown Princess* burned up in Xenobe's atmosphere fifteen minutes ago. Everyone aboard was lost."

"Merrick and Keller gone," Peters said slowly. "Along with my best officer, and your Ms. Shadow."

MacKenzie's mouth worked but no sound came forth. After a moment he turned away.

Ti-ling, poised at Peters' shoulder, shook herself as if awakening from some long strange dream. Peering at the screen with newfound interest, she said slowly, "Did I hear you say that Merrick is gone?"

"Yes."

"Are you certain?"

"We won't know for sure until we recover the space buoy evidence. But he was seen entering that ship, in pursuit of Kate Shadow."

Ti-ling gasped.

Peters reached out to comfort her.

She shook him off. A radiant smile spread across her face. "Gone," she said. "The bastard is really gone."

Iger felt as though he would fly apart, as though

the top of his head might explode. Kate dead? Dead in some stupid accident that could have been avoided? Running off, as she always did, only this time she wasn't coming back, ever.

His eyes fell upon Ti-ling and suddenly his sorrow turned to anger. *That's it, bitch,* he thought. *Smile. The woman I love is dead, and so is your business partner.* And Iger froze at the thought. Ti-ling had been Merrick's partner. Did Darius Peters know that? How could he?

Casually, Iger leaned toward the tiny woman. "That's no way to act," he said. "Merrick was your friend."

Ti-ling pulled back. "What do you mean?"

"I mean that you were in with him on the mindsalt schemes, weren't you?"

"How . . . absurd," she said. "He was a monster. I hated the man. I had nothing to do with him."

But the damage had been done. A tiny flame of suspicion had ignited in Darius Peters' eyes. "Those are serious statements, son. Libelous."

"I've got proof," Iger said. He had the cube recording from the bug that Katie had planted upon "Keller" when she had sent him to see Merrick. He would bring it to Peters.

"Darius, he's lying!" Ti-ling's eyes flashed at Iger, green venom in their ebony depths.

Iger shook his head. "Check the registry on all the mindsalt mines of Styx," he said quietly. "Look under new listings. Then tell me that I'm lying." He stood up and, without another word, walked toward the door. He had done his best. Let Peters look after his own business. Iger wanted to be alone and mourn his dead.

* * *

Lyle MacKenzie excused himself from the room as the discussion between Darius Peters and Ti-ling grew heated. He had no desire to be an audience to their private battles.

Stepping outside, MacKenzie thought that he, too, would like some time to digest the bad news, to attempt to deal with Kate's death.

He was halfway home when he heard them: Hurried footsteps, getting louder, closer.

Something told MacKenzie that he wasn't going to get the time to mourn Kate properly.

He reached for his disruptor and hurried into a vacant shop to hide and see who was following him.

The door slammed open. Cristobal stood there holding a laser pistol.

"Outside," he rasped. "Now!"

"Cristobal . . ."

"I don't want to hear what you have to say. I won't listen!" Absurdly he cupped one hand over his ear, holding the gun on MacKenzie with the other. "You're lying, whatever you say. I don't care."

MacKenzie realized that he was going to have to kill him. Darius Peters had been right all along.

"Merrick lied to me," Cristobal said. "He told me he didn't have any mindsalt left. But he did, he did. And I found it. When I heard that he went up in that ship, I broke into his apartment. I found the salt. I found it and I took it."

"How much?"

"All there was."

Feverishly, MacKenzie imagined Cristobal swallowing mindsalt. He was out of his head, completely crazed now. No use trying to reason with him.

Cristobal babbled on. "Keller was supposed to be dead. But he's alive. He'll tell everybody I blew up Brayton's Rock, I know he will. But I was only doing what he wanted."

"What about betraying the War Minstrels?"

"I didn't want to! Katie made me do it. If she hadn't stolen control, I wouldn't have had to do it. But she was power-hungry, do you see? The bitch wanted everything. Everything! What's she got now, but cold stars?" He laughed, a sound halfway between mirth and despair.

"Cristobal . . ."

"Shut up! Bastard, always reminding me of the past. Always telling everybody that I screwed your sister. Took bribes. Sold favors. So what?"

"It's never your fault, is it?"

"You don't understand. You never did, Mac."

"I think you'd better shoot me here. I'm getting tired of walking."

"Move, damn you."

"No."

Cristobal's face screwed up as though he were about to cry.

MacKenzie slugged him, hard, in the gut.

With a groan, Cristobal crumpled. But he managed to lash out and grab one of MacKenzie's feet, sending him sprawling. The two of them rolled over and over across the hard stones of the plaza, locked together in hostile embrace, neither yielding. MacKenzie felt his head being wrenched back toward the ground. He got a leg under his adversary's knee and flipped them both around so that he had the advantage.

But the mindsalt gave Cristobal a frenzied strength. Twice he threw MacKenzie off, and twice MacKenzie, with desperate effort, managed to grab hold of him again,

Thwack!

Cristobal's forehead crashed against MacKenzie's face, nearly flattening his nose, sending sparks of pain flaring into his eyes. Blood began to stream down MacKenzie's cheeks, dyeing the front of his stretchsuit deep vermilion.

He gave Cristobal a pounding chop that sent him back and down with such force that MacKenzie feared he had cracked his opponent's skull against the pavement.

No such luck. Cristobal thrashed, cursing, beneath him. Somehow he got an arm around MacKenzie's neck and began trying to press MacKenzie's head over it.

The son-of-a-bitch really is trying to kill me, MacKenzie thought. *This fight is absolutely to the death.*

The thought galvanized him, gave him a fierce desire to be finished and done with Cristobal. MacKenzie remembered that he had tucked a small vibroblade into his back pocket. If he could just reach it and press the trigger . . .

Strong hands laid hold of him and pulled him off Cristobal even as he fumbled for the knife with which to kill him.

Screaming wildly, helplessly, Cristobal was being similarly restrained.

MacKenzie's vision was clouded by blood. He couldn't see who had interfered in the fight. As he began to protest, he felt somebody wiping his face. At the same time, a gloriously familiar voice said, "I can't turn my back on you for a minute, can I?"

"Katie!" He stared, disbelieving. Then, heedless of the blood, he threw his arms around her. "I thought you were dead. Iger told me that the ship you took had burned up."

"It did. I just didn't happen to be on it when it did."

"But how?"

For answer she gestured behind her and pulled

back. He could see familiar figures standing all around him. Some of them were holding Cristobal: Rab, Arsobades, and Salome. They looked thin and ragged, on the whole, worse for wear. But all three of them were grinning.

MacKenzie staggered forward to grasp hands. "Well met," he said. "Well met indeed. But how?"

"They found me in space, with Lt. Sherno," Katie said. "Showed up in the nick of time."

"Sherno?" MacKenzie's smile widened. "He survived, too?"

"Both of us."

"They were jsut hanging around," Arsobades said. "Didn't seem to have anything better to do."

Rab chimed in. "And we happened to be in the neighborhood. Seemed like bad manners to just leave them there with their oxygen running out."

"What about the others?" MacKenzie said. "Keller? Merrick the Blackbird?"

The expression in Salome's amber eyes turned grim and the lines in her dark face deepened as she shook her head and said softly, "We were too late for them."

"They never had a chance," Rab added. "They were finished as soon as that lock blew. A bad spacer's death, sucked out of the ship without pressure suits."

At his words MacKenzie felt a chill run through him. So the man who had been gunning for him, his former colleague in revolution, was truly dead, suffocated in space. The news should have given him a sense of relief. But all he felt was horror.

Gingerly he checked himself for damage. His nose hurt. His jaw ached. He probed his teeth with his tongue and found to his relief that none of them seemed to have been dislodged.

"What about the mindsalt?" he asked.

"Gone," Katie said. "The holds blew. The whole load of it went into space, right behind Merrick."

"Best place for it."

Katie gave him an unreadable look.

"That should put an end to it," Salome said.

"Not quite," Katie said. "Not until we stop Ti-ling. She was in on the mines with Merrick."

"That cinches it," MacKenzie said. "Cozying up to Darius Peters on one hand and working with Merrick on the other. That woman has brass."

"Ti-ling?" With a frenzied gasp, Cristobal broke free of Arsobades' grasp. "She thought she would keep me out of it, didn't she? Where is she? I'll show that bitch. I'll—"

But whatever threat he might have issued died in his throat. A spasm took hold of Cristobal and shook him, hard. His legs locked in place, knees quivering. A thin trickle of saliva leaked from the corner of his mouth and his eyes rolled upward in his head. Shaking, his arms rigid at his sides, he fell backward, hitting the pavement headfirst with a sickening thud. And stopped shaking.

Arsobades knelt quickly beside him and pressed two fingers against Cristobal's slack throat. Then he shook his head.

"Dead?" Even as he said it MacKenzie knew that it wasn't a question. "He was hopped up on mind-salt. Crazy."

"His heart must have quit on him," said Rab. "Most likely he was dead before his head even hit the ground."

For a moment no one spoke. Then Katie said, "He cheated death for a long, long time. I'd say that Cristobal's luck just ran out, finally.

Chapter Twenty-Three

The bar was dim, smoky, and relatively empty. Its name was something like "Natural Selection." Iger couldn't quite remember. Not that it was important.

His determination to be alone had lasted only until he walked past the first tavern in Vardalia's Tanveil District. Normally he would have been a bit choosier. But all he wanted a dark place to hide and drink until he passed out. The Natural Selection had a nice cool ledge against which he could rest his forehead.

It might have been perfect, at least temporarily, if only the blasted mechband hadn't kept droning that same damned song, over and over:

"Walking through the shadows,
I think of you.
Standing in the shadows,
I think of you.
Baby, why'd you leave me?
Baby, where did you go?

Walking through the shadows,
I gotta know."

After the fifth repeat, Iger said to no one in particular, "Can you stop that goddamn thing?"

The barkeep shrugged. "The owner likes it. Reminds him of his ex-wife."

"His ex-wife, you say?" Iger sighed. This was worse than he thought. There was just no reasoning with men about their ex-wives. He pulled out his laser pistol, aimed carefully, and blasted the band several times. Pieces of blue and purple ceramsteel flew around the room, embedding themselves in the walls. The music came to an abrupt halt.

"Hey!" the barkeep yelled. "What's the hell's the matter with you?"

Iger pulled a wad of credits out of his pocket and set them down in a puddle of beer. "Here. There's enough there to buy two more mechbands. Three, if you buy used."

Eyeing the roll of money, the barkeep had an obvious change of heart. "Hey, buddy," he said, grinning. "I got a brother-in-law you can shoot for nothing."

"I don't like shooting people." As Iger said it, he thought of Yates Keller. Well, he wouldn't have minded shooting that bastard, might even have enjoyed it, actually. But now he'd never have the chance.

Morosely he downed another Red Jack. Later, he

knew, he was going to have a miserable sick headache—beer hangovers were the worst of all. But he didn't care. He didn't care about anything right now except not thinking and drowning his heartache.

A sharp-faced woman with long dark hair set into greasy spirals—a hooker?—leaned up against the counter and pressed her knee into his. "You keep that up, you'll need a gurney to get you out of here."

"Thanks, Mom."

The hooker flashed him a dark murderous glare and sullenly moved on.

Green eyes, he thought.

Katie had green eyes, too.

Iger felt his lower lip begin to tremble. The lump in his chest began to move up into his throat. In a moment, he suspected, he was going to lose it completely, break down right here in the bar and weep like an infant.

He turned his head away, wiped his nose against his sleeve, and heard a familiar voice say, "You could've at least waited for me before you started celebrating."

He whirled.

Red hair, green eyes.

"Katie?"

Oh, gods, it was her. But she was dead.

There was only one explanation.

He was hallucinating. Losing his mind. "Go

away," he said thickly. "You're dead. I've had it up to here with ghosts. Get out of here."

"You ninny. I'm no ghost."

He covered his ears and began humming.

Whack!

He looked at her, astonished. "You slapped my head!"

"I'll do more than that if you don't stop acting like an idiot."

No ghost, then. It was Kate, his own Katie, returned from the dead and wearing her familiar impatient expression. A miracle. Iger stared at her, felt the blood flowing through his veins, and in that moment was seized by one complete, electrifying emotion.

Fury.

"Goddamn you, Kate!" He got to his feet, weaving slightly. "I've had it."

"Iger, you're drunk."

"Yeah, I am. But not too drunk to know that I'm fed up. You're always going off and getting yourself imprisoned or shot or possessed or blown up or whatever and then coming back and expecting me to be sitting somewhere quietly, knitting with Third Child and waiting."

"Don't be ridiculous."

He went storming on, oblivious to her comments. "Or your mind gets trapped in somebody else's body. Not to worry. Good old Iger will take care of you until your mind comes back, won't he? Of course he will. Got a mindghost caught in your noggin? No problem. Iger doesn't mind three-in-a-bed. Iger doesn't mind three-in-a-head. Good old Iger."

"Iger—"

"Don't interrupt me. You can just go off next time and get killed and come back without me, Kate. I'm tired of playing second fiddle to your schemes and revolutions, your Mindstars and enemies. I've had it!"

He stomped toward the door. Paused, drew himself up with all the dignity he could muster. "Are you reading my mind now? If you are, you'll see that I'm telling you to go to hell!" He made a rude gesture and proudly sauntered out the door.

* * *

On the street outside the Natural Selection, Kayla peered, speechless, after her lover.

Iger was getting farther away all the time.

She watched him and thought, *Let him go. Who needs him? I don't need anybody.*

She remembered tumbling through the vacuum up above St. Ilban, just another object in the massive void. She watched the planets spin in their stately dance, each of them moving away from her like Iger.

If he feels that way, then good ridddance!

And the next thought: *Sister Blood doesn't need anybody. Never has.*

Sister Blood, Sister Blood, Sister Blood.

She could hear Golias' last anguished screams as she let him float away.

She saw the planets in their endless peaceful waltz around the green and yellow suns.

Peace. That was what Kayla wanted. Her anger had burned away. Her enemies were dead and gone. Peace, yes. She didn't want to fight any longer. Instead, she felt a great desire to come to earth, to rest, to halt all furious motion. And with that compelling desire came the longing to create instead of destroy.

Keller was finished. Merrick, too. If there were any scores left unsettled, Kayla didn't want to know about them. She wasn't interested in the future thoughts of Sister Blood.

Peace.

And suddenly Kayla was running, sprinting down the street after the receding figure of her lover.

"Iger," she cried. "Iger, wait!"

He had gotten a damned good lead on her.

She chased him most of the way back to Vardalia Port. Finally he was within hailing distance. She stopped, gasping for breath, heart pounding.

"Iger, wait."

"No way."

"Dammit, slow down at least."

He didn't pause for a moment. "Why don't you just use your fancy mindpowers to stun me?"

The Kayla of times past might have done just that,

might have pulled her mindpowers together and given him a jolt to remember before she blistered him with a few choice, final comments and left. Instead, she merely said, "Don't tempt me."

He paused and turned to look at her, and his mouth quirked as if he were fighting back a smile.

Kayla covered the distance between them in two bounds, threw her arms around him, kissed him deeply. Then she pulled back to stare into his blue eyes.

"You idiot," she said. "I really love you."

His expression was wary. "You do?"

"Yeah, I do."

He squinted at her. "Are you drunk?"

"No, you are."

Iger shook his head. "Well, I'm sorry, but I'm not used to this. A public demonstration of affection."

"Better get used to it."

"What's up? What do you want?"

"Let's get married," she said.

"Are you serious?"

"Never more so."

A slow smile spread across Iger's face. "Married? You mean it? For real?"

"Yeah. Let's make an honest dalkoi of Third Child."

Iger chuckled. "Sounds good to me."

"Me, too." And she kissed him again, before he could change his mind.

* * *

Hand in hand, Kayla and Iger walked into Darius Peters' office in the Police Ministry.

Ti-ling, Darius Peters, and Lyle MacKenzie were gathered by the window, staring out at Vardalia in all of its tattered glory. Nearby, Rab, Salome, and Arsobades were settled into wallseats. Arsobades was fiddling with a mechlute. The sight made Kayla smile broadly.

"Here she is at last," Rab said in his raspy growl. "Her Highness, newly returned from the near-dead, has finally deigned to arrive." He bowed his head in mock obeisance.

Kayla gave him a disgusted look. "Stow it, Rab. I'm here, aren't I? What's all the fuss?"

With a nod in Darius Peters' direction, Rab said, "Ask him. He's the one who called this meeting."

"Yes," Peters said. "I want to discuss a proposal that Ti-ling's made."

"About what?"

"About mindsalt. The mindsalt trade, and how it can benefit Vardalia."

Kayla stared at the small woman with suspicion. "Benefit Vardalia?" Had Darius Peters lost his mind? No, he was merely under the influence of a very potent drug: love.

Nodding with self-assurance, Ti-ling took center stage. "Yes. Darius and I have discussed it thoroughly, and he agrees that the wisest thing to do is run the Styx mines as a cooperative. The profits from the sales of mindstones and salt could be used to help rebuild this city."

"And what about the effects on the users of mindsalt?" Arsobades said. "What benefits will they get?"

Ti-liing turned wide and guileless eyes upon the minstrel. "No one puts a gun to their heads and tells them to take the drug, much less to misuse it."

"But you'll admit that your scheme hinges upon the sales of the drug?" Rab said.

"Of course." Ti-ling seemed irritated by Rab's emphasis on such minor details.

As she spoke, from out of Kayla's memory came an image of a vast silvery serpent encircling St. Ilban, a human/serpent with her face. Then its visage blurred, shifted, to become Pelleas Karlson, Yates Keller, Merrick the Blackbird. And Ti-ling. So many different familiar features, composite faces, each one with its mouth open. The serpent devoured St. Ilban and turned, stretching across space, reaching for Styx, teeth sharp and ready.

No, Kayla thought. *No. No. No..*

Now she saw the face of Yates Keller, beseeching her to save him, not to consign him to the vacuum, to death. Yates Keller and all of his murderous knowledge, newly inhabited by Golias, a mindghost eager to exploit Keller's memories, to seize power and exploit it ruthlessly.

The stones poisoned all who came in contact with them. It was inevitable.

But Ti-ling's voice cut into her thoughts: "And let's not forget the groupmind. There's the possibility of applying it to healing works. A well-run groupmind. It doesn't have to be a bad, dangerous thing. Look at the dalkoi and how they use their combined empathic powers."

Kayla listened to Ti-ling's words and yearned to silence the woman's yattering. She mistrusted this scheme. Mindsalt didn't simply hurt, it damaged. It scarred. It had to be stopped.

Again she felt the desire to create and preserve instead of destroy, and a growing determination to end the malignant effects of the mindsalt trade.

But how is this not destroying? she wondered. *How is this not the destruction of what my parents, and their parents before them, worked so hard for, even died for?*

They hadn't known that the things they dug from the living rock, hour by hour, sweating in the dark, the mindstones they strove so desperately for, were ultimately destroying people. They had simply wanted to put food on the table, to care for their families.

But the mindstones and salt hurt, maimed, and killed. They drew men and women to their destruction and death. Made mindslaves, zombies, and—she thought of Pelleas Karlson—turned the merely corrupt into something truly monstrous. Mindsalt was the ruination of entire planets.

By putting an end to the mindstone and mindsalt trade she would be bringing a halt to the long, sad process that had begun in her parents' mines and ended far away in the empty wreckage of people's lives and the degradation of cities.

It had to be stopped. And by ending destruction wasn't she creating a beginning of sorts?

Yes. Yes.

Resolve sharpened within her. Enough. No more mindsalt, now or ever.

She looked around the room at the people there, those whom she knew well and loved, and the others toward whom she at least felt no enmity. "I have a better idea," Kayla said.

They stared at her expectantly.

Salome leaned forward, her amber eyes intent. "What do you mean, Katie?"

Taking an extra-deep breath, Kayla said, "Shut it all down. The mines, the stones, the salt, every bit of it, the whole damned thing. Give anybody on-planet the option of leaving: send shuttles, whatever. But shut it all down. Shut it down and throw away the key."

Darius Peters cleared his throat. "That's your determination?" he asked.

"That's it. Shut down the mines. I want them

stopped once and for all. Sealed. Destroyed, if necessary."

"No!" Ti-ling cried. "You're crazy." She clutched at Peters in supplication. "Darius, don't pay any attention to her. It's a marvelous system. It just needs to be administered properly."

"Marvelous?" Lyle MacKenzie's eyes went wide. "How can you call a system that enslaves people and destroys their lives marvelous? Have you forgotten that it reduced this city to rubble?"

Ti-ling gestured impatiently. "Don't be melodramatic. Whatever damage was done can all be restored. What's important is that the information not be lost. Don't you see? Pelly built it all. The framework. Studied the mindstones and learned all of their wonderful secrets."

"Wonderful?" Now Arsobades and Rab were staring at the tiny woman in amazement.

"Darius." A pleading note entered Ti-ling's voice. She was looking only at Peters now, as though no one else were in the room. "Don't you see it? Oh, please, broaden your horizons, darling. Together we could manage it. Become the administrators, the rulers of the system. We were meant to do it."

Darius Peters had the thunderstruck expression of a man who has just awakened from a beautiful dream and discovered that he has stepped into a nightmare. "You were just using me," Peters said slowly. "The entire time. You never cared for me, never cared at all."

"No, no! You've got it all wrong. Darius, please, listen to me. At first I intended to just use you, yes, I won't deny that. But I've come to care for you, Darius. Really care. Please believe me." She held out her hand. "We'll do it all together. With what I know of the stones, and your control of the police, nothing can possibly go wrong. It can be a perfect system. Please open your mind."

"Ti-ling." His voice was soft but his expression was something else. Slowly he shook his head.

"You're all such small people," Ti-ling said disgustedly. "Pelly wasn't. He had vision. Great visions."

Carefully Darius Peters extracted his hand from Ti-ling's grip. "Out," he said. "Get out."

"But, darling . . ."

"Not another word. Go. Just go." Peters' eyes flashed with murderous intent.

Ti-ling stared at him a long moment as though she were unable to believe the evidence of her own ears. Then she pulled her silken cloak about her and, head held high, walked out of the room, trailing perfume.

Darius Peters leaned heavily upon his desk. His eyes were wells of pain.

For a moment no one spoke. Then Peters seemed to master his distress. Shaking his head sadly he pressed another button and his deskscreen came to live.

"Notify all squadron leaders," he said. "We'll be sending an evacuation force to Styx. An evacuation force and a warship. See that there are appropriate escorts. Lyle MacKenzie will coordinate. And if Lt. Commander Sherno has sufficiently recovered from his latest adventure, tell him that I'd like him to head up the Styx forces."

Kayla nodded. That was the right answer. Evacuate Styx and seal it, forever. Lock it up and throw away the key, and forbid any mention of it.

The image of her home world came to her, of the small red planet that contained so many of her old memories—both sweet and sour—locked tightly, forever. It was oddly appealing.

Her old crewmates from the *Falstaff* were nodding, practically cheering their approval.

There was a long silence in the room. It was broken, at last, by Rab. "So, Katie," he said. He spoke in a loud voice, exaggeratedly hearty. "What's next, eh? Ready to mount up and ride with us? You and Iger?"

Kayla smiled. "I thought you didn't want anything more to do with us." She was amused to see the *Falstaff*'s burly first mate wince with embarrassment.

"Let's say that we rethought that policy," Rab said quickly. "We were fools to blame you—goddamn fools."

"Out of our heads, absolutely," Arsobades added. "You were right about that."

Salome smiled quietly. "And that's why we came back."

"Good timing," Kayla said dryly.

"So your forgive us?" Rab said.

"Don't be ridiculous."

Salome lifted clear amber eyes to meet hers. "Your bunk on the *Falstaff* is ready for you whenever you want it."

Regret stabbed at Kayla as she said, quietly, calmly, "I'm afraid that's just not possible."

"Damned straight," MacKenzie said. "Kate's going to have her hands full around here, helping me make sense out of this godforsaken city." He turned and gave her a dazzling smile, half relief, half triumph.

"Oh, Mac. I'm sorry. I wish I could."

MacKenzie's smile faded. "But, Katie, you've got to stay here and help me administer this place." He sounded more than a little desperate. "Now that Merrick's gone and Cristobal, too, we've got to put this place together. And you're a necessary part of the job. The people will listen to you."

"They'll listen to you, too. You and Darius Peters. I've got other plans."

MacKenzie looked as though he would burst. "But—Vardalia. What about Vardalia?"

"Vardalia will manage," said Kayla. "With or without my help. Seems to me that you and Darius

Peters are putting it on the right track. I don't have any doubt that you'll sort it out. It just takes time."

"But you fought so hard for it. We all did."

"I don't want this place, Mac. I never really did. I fixed on Vardalia and the revolution as ways to achieve my revenge. But that wasn't what I wanted at all."

He stared at her, obviously astounded. "Not want it? Not want the War Minstrels? The cause? Pardon me for asking, Kate N. Shadow, but if you didn't want Vardalia, just what in nine hells did you want?"

Kayla smiled gently, leaned across to take Iger's hand. Holding it up, she said, "This. This is what I wanted, nothing but this. But I didn't know it. I thought I had to get revenge for my parents' deaths. And that I should make Yates Keller pay for his crimes, and, by extension, anybody associated with him. And that I had to get the *Falstaff* out of debt, and lead the War Minstrels to Vardalia. All those things."

They were all staring at her.

"Don't you see, Mac? I thought I wanted speed and thunder, war and blood feud. But I was wrong. What I wanted was love. Just that, nothing more. Connection. Life. I'm finished with looking backward."

She squeezed Iger's hand and got an answering squeeze in return. "I can't stay here in Vardalia. I want to be with Third Child when she has her baby.

And perhaps I'd like to contemplate other births as well."

Iger smiled slyly.

"So we're going to go back to Liage," Kayla said.

"Liage?" MacKenzie said.

"Liage?" Rab echoed.

Salome wrinkled her elegant nose. "To that prairie? All you'll have there is grass and more grass."

Rab looked completely mystified. "What are you planning to do, raise bambera? Become erfani wranglers?"

"Maybe. Or perhaps we'll seek out the dalkoi, learn their healing techniques, their special mind-powers. Ti-ling was right about that. Maybe I'll learn all about them and, in time, bring that knowledge back."

Iger gave her a look of pleased surprise.

"I think they have a great deal to teach us," Kayla said. "I'm sure of it."

"Third Child would agree with you," Iger said. "It's a good thing she's not here. That dalkoi's getting a swelled head as it is."

Salome and Rab were gaping at both of them as though they thought that insanity might be an infectious disease. But Arsobades was smiling. Smiling and nodding. "Good for you, Katie," he said. "It's a fine plan. Maybe I'll even come visit you one of these days."

Kayla threw him a grateful look.

"Just one more thing," she said. "My name. It's not Kate Shadow. It's Kayla. Kayla John Reed."

She hugged Rab, Arsobades, Salome, and even MacKenzie, and shook hands with Darius Peters.

"Good luck," she told him. "I think Vardalia has finally gotten the kind of leaders it needs. Take good care of it."

With her good-byes said, her anger gone, and Sister Blood dead and buried, Kayla had the rest of her life to explore and discover. It spread before her, beckoning.

Smiling at Iger, she said, "Come on. Let's collect Third Child and go home."

Kate Elliott

The Novels of the Jaran:

☐ **JARAN: Book 1** UE2513—$5.99
Here is the poignant and powerful story of a young woman's coming of age on an alien world, where she is both player and pawn in an interstellar game of intrigue and politics.

☐ **AN EARTHLY CROWN: Book 2** UE2546—$5.99
The jaran people, led by Ilya Bakhtiian and his Earth-born wife Tess, are sweeping across the planet Rhui on a campaign of conquest. But even more important is the battle between Ilya and Duke Charles, Tess' brother, who is ruler of this sector of space.

☐ **HIS CONQUERING SWORD: Book 3** UE2551—$5.99
Even as Jaran warlord Ilya continues the conquest of his world, he faces a far more dangerous power struggle with his wife's brother, leader of an underground human rebellion against the alien empire.

☐ **THE LAW OF BECOMING: Book 4** UE2580—$5.99
On Rhui, Ilya's son inadvertently becomes the catalyst for what could prove a major shift of power. And in the heart of the empire, the most surprising move of all was about to occur as the Emperor added an unexpected new player to the Game of Princes . . .

Buy them at your local bookstore or use this convenient coupon for ordering.

PENGUIN USA P.O. Box 999—Dep. #17109, Bergenfield, New Jersey 07621

Please send me the DAW BOOKS I have checked above, for which I am enclosing $______________ (please add $2.00 to cover postage and handling). Send check or money order (no cash or C.O.D.'s) or charge by Mastercard or VISA (with a $15.00 minimum). Prices and numbers are subject to change without notice.

Card #______________________ Exp. Date ______________________
Signature____
Name____
Address____
City ______________________ State ______________ Zip Code ______________

For faster service when ordering by credit card call **1-800-253-6476**

Allow a minimum of 4-6 weeks for delivery. This offer is subject to change without notice.

Lisanne Norman

☐ **TURNING POINT** UE2575—$3.99

When a human-colonized world falls under the sway of aliens who have already enslaved many another race, there is scant hope of salvation from far-distant Earth. Instead, their hopes rest upon an underground rebellion and the intervention of a team of catlike aliens, one of whom links with a young woman gifted with unique mind powers.

☐ **FORTUNE'S WHEEL** UE2675—$5.99

Carrie was the daughter of the human governor of the colony planet Keiss. Kusac was the son and heir of the Sholan Clan Lord. Both were telepaths and the bond they formed was compounded equally of love and mind power. But now they were about to be thrust into the heart of an interstellar conflict, as factions on both their worlds sought to use the duo's powers for their own ends . . .

☐ **FIRE MARGINS** UE2718—$6.99

A new race is about to be born on the Sholan homeworld, and it may cause the current unstable political climate to explode. Only through exploring the Sholan's long-buried and purposely forgotten past can Carrie and Kusac hope to find the path to survival, not only for their own people, but for Sholans and humans as well.
